"You should have told Teresa the truth."

Sharley continued, "It's unkind to let her believe you married me because of my connections."

"Is that what she told you?" Marcos looked at her in surprise.

"She delighted in telling me so," Sharley emphasized. "And also in warning me that my marriage won't last."

They walked in silence, then Marcos said suddenly, "I felt I had to give her some explanation of why I married you so suddenly. Teresa is a simple girl, pretty and uncomplicated."

"Uncomplicated as a fox! Once she's married to you she'll lead you by the nose."

"I have yet to meet the woman capable of that," he stated coolly.

Sharley tossed her head. "I'd love to see her crack the whip."

"When that time comes," he replied swiftly, "you won't be here."

RACHEL LINDSAY
is also the author of these

Harlequin Presents

and these

Harlequin Romances

Many of these titles are available at your local bookseller.

For a free catalogue listing all available Harlequin Romances
and Harlequin Presents, send your name and address to:

HARLEQUIN READER SERVICE
1440 South Priest Drive, Tempe, AZ 85281
Canadian address: Stratford, Ontario N5A 6W2

RACHEL LINDSAY

untouched wife

Harlequin Books

TORONTO • LONDON • LOS ANGELES • AMSTERDAM
SYDNEY • HAMBURG • PARIS • STOCKHOLM • ATHENS • TOKYO

Harlequin Presents edition published November 1981
ISBN 0-373-10467-7

Original hardcover edition published in 1981
by Mills & Boon Limited

CHAPTER ONE

CHARLOTTE BOSWELL put down the telephone receiver and wished she could strangle the man at the other end of it. What pleasure it would give her to do so! But unfortunately she had no hope of achieving her ambition. Indeed, it was his refusal to see her which had aroused her anger in the first place. Who did Marcos Santana think he was, to be so scathing about the *Weekly News'* request to interview him?

'I have no wish to be featured in your kind of newspaper,' he had said coldly. 'I appreciate that your readers are interested in what I am doing, but their curiosity is of no concern to me or to my company.'

'It isn't *your* company our readers are curious about,' Sharley had retorted. 'But since you're hoping to become partners with an important *British* company——'

'Then I suggest you contact *them.*'

Before Charlotte could think of a reply, the man had abruptly rung off, leaving her to acknowledge that her careful research during the past two weeks had been a total waste of time. Damn Marcos Santana! she thought furiously. It would be easier to see the Pope. His suggestion that she contact Fawcett and Lloyd, the British company with whom he was negotiating, was no solution to her problem. Her main interest was the human angle: Marcos Santana, himself.

She was fascinated by his determination to remain head of the Santana Wine Company, which his great-great-grandfather had founded, and she was convinced that an interview with him, should she ever succeed in getting one, would make a wonderful story.

He had first come to her attention when he had skilfully outwitted the group of dissident workers who had tried to gain control of his company; 'brilliant strategist' was but one of the comments made about him in the London financial papers, which had then gone on to extol his decision to amalgamate with the largest and most important wine importers in Britain.

A news item in a London evening paper, saying he had flown in from Oporto, had prompted her to get in touch with him through the Vice-Consul at his Embassy, and the young diplomat had been so co-operative that Charlotte was unprepared for Marcos Santana's cold response.

'What's wrong, Sharley? Won't the Queen see you?' The question came from Frank Fox, a plump young man in his thirties who occupied the desk next to hers in the large, open-plan office of the *Weekly News*.

Sharley grinned, recognising the teasing as admiration of her ability to get interviews with the most inaccessible people.

'As a matter of fact, there *is* someone who won't see me. His high and mightyship Marcos Santana.'

Frank recognised the name and pulled a face.

'Pity. It would have been a good story. I had a drink with a friend at the *Telegraph* yesterday and he said they're running a big feature on Pedro Lopez, the fellow who's been trying to overthrow Santana. Why don't you go to Lisbon to see *him* instead?'

'Because I'm not prepared to do a biased interview. I know Lopez would love to talk his head off, but I'll only see him if I can also see Santana.'

Sharley rose from behind her desk, a tall, extremely slender girl redeemed from being too thin by firm, full breasts and delicately curving hips. She had a svelteness that drew all male eyes—a fact to which three years as an ace reporter on the *Weekly News* had made her accustomed—and she walked the length of the room with self-assurance, her steps fluid, her long, fair hair swinging back as she moved. Today she wore a cream silk shirt and flared brown skirt, the hem lifting slightly around legs which still managed to look shapely in low-heeled shoes.

Reaching the corridor, she hurried towards the editor's office and, after a short wait, was sitting in front of Sam Morris's desk. It was as tidy as the man was untidy, yet she knew that the mind behind the shaggy appearance was rapier-sharp.

'So what do you expect *me* to do?' he asked, when she had told him of her difficulty in seeing Santana. 'No one's yet managed to get an interview with him.'

'Won't you at least try? Pull a few strings, Sam. *Please!*'

Signalling her to remain where she was, he picked up his private telephone. After making several calls he put down the receiver and scowled at her.

'No dice. The Senhor is successfully playing hard to get. You'd better find yourself someone else to interview.'

'I suppose I could phone my godfather,' Sharley reflected. 'I don't like asking him for any favours, but——'

'My God!' Sam Morris exploded. 'I'd forgotten who your godfather was. And you had the nerve to ask *me* to pull strings! Phone him at once girl, or I'll fire you.'

Grinning at the threat; for she knew it to be an idle one, Sharley dialled the number of Sir George Fawcett.

As she had expected, she was put through to his secretary, but the moment she gave her name he came on the line.

'Anything wrong?' he asked at once, for she rarely called him at his office.

'Not personally,' she said reassuringly. 'But I'm trying to get an interview with Marcos Santana and he's being impossible.

Her godfather chuckled. 'So you want me to arrange it, eh?'

'Would you?' she pleaded. 'But don't tell him I'm your goddaughter, and don't mention my name, because he knows it.'

'I'll just say it's a top Fleet Street reporter from the *News*,' her godfather reassured her. 'Though if you'd told him you knew me, I'm sure he would have seen you.'

'I don't like parading my illustrious relations,' Sharley said.

Sir George laughed. 'I could appreciate you hiding it if you were seeing that Lopez fellow, but Santana is a friend of mine. And talking about friends, Madge wants to know when you're going to stop ignoring us and pay us a visit.'

'When she stops trying to matchmake,' Sharley replied promptly. 'But I'll give her a call and arrange to come down for a weekend.'

'Good. Now if you'll hold on a moment I'll have a word with Santana. I came out of a meeting with him to take this call.'

'Oh, Uncle George, I *am* sorry. I didn't know.'

She balanced the receiver on her shoulder and gave the thumbs-up sign to her editor.

'What it is to have illustrious relations,' he murmured from behind a foul-smelling pipe. 'I must remember to familiarize myself with your blue-blooded stock.'

The jangle of heavy gold bracelets was Sharley's only answer as she raised a slender arm to push away her hair from her face. As she did so, her godfather came back on the line to say that Marcos Santana would see her at three-thirty that afternoon in his apartment in St James's.

'You're an angel,' Sharley said in delight. 'When I write the story, is there anything you'd like me to say about *your* company?'

'Just spell our name right,' he replied, and with a laugh hung up.

'I might get you to do a piece on Sir George one day,' Sam Morris said.

'I never write about people I know personally.' She went to the door. 'Will you put the Santana story in tomorrow?'

'Let me see it first. If I like it, it might do for a big feature on Friday.'

Sharley nodded and went out, pleased by the prospect of getting the extra space that a feature article on Friday would mean.

Promptly to time that afternoon, she rang the doorbell of the apartment in the discreetly opulent block which stood within walking distance of Green Park. No one answered her ring and she put her finger on the bell and kept it there for several seconds.

Suddenly the door was swung open by a manservant. He looked at Sharley impassively, but because she knew she was expected, she started to cross the threshold. At once he blocked her way. 'You no come in.'

'I have an appointment with Senhor Santana.' From her handbag she took out her Press card. 'Will you please tell him the reporter from the *Weekly News* is here.'

Surprise crossed the manservant's face, but he politely asked her to wait, then disappeared through the door behind him, closing it shut.

Barely had thirty seconds passed when the door was flung open again and Sharley found herself face to face with the man she had wanted to strangle earlier that morning.

He had the thick, shiny black hair and finely chiselled features of most aristocratic Portuguese, but in all other respects he was completely different from what she had anticipated. Firstly, there was his height, which was well over six feet. Then there was the graceful way he moved: a fluid motion of the body that made her think that here was no dynamic businessman but someone who looked as if he would be more at home in the world of ballet or art. He even had a handkerchief tucked into his sleeve, and she would not have been surprised to see him stop and take out a snuffbox. Yes, there was something very much of the Scarlet Pimpernel about him, except that the Pimpernel's effeteness had disguised steely strength, while this man looked genuinely languid and bored.

Then Sharley remembered their sharp verbal exchange on the telephone this morning, and the fact that Marcos Santana was in the process of concluding a successful agreement with her godfather, who would never consider joining forces with a man he did not respect, no matter how much he wanted that man's business. That meant only one thing: in no way was Marcos Santana as languid as the impression he gave.

Sharley's interest stirred and she gave him a firm smile. 'Good afternoon, Senhor Santana. Sir George Fawcett was kind enough to arrange for me to see you.'

'*You* are the reporter he mentioned?' His English was impeccable and the voice so low and soft that only the faintest hint of an accent could be heard, more in the intonation than in the words themselves. 'Sir George did not tell me it was a woman.'

'He probably didn't think it necessary.'

'It was very necessary. Had I known, I would never have agreed to it.'

Sharley was not used to this kind of attitude.

'I am not here as a woman, Senhor Santana, but as a reporter who happens to *be* a woman.'

'Such play with words does not convince me. You are both a woman and a reporter and, as such, I have no intention of allowing you to interview me. I do not wish to be portrayed in your women's pages. I am in England solely for business reasons and there is no need for me to become known to your readers.'

'Many of my readers happen to be your customers, *senhor*. That alone should make it worth your while to reconsider what you've said.'

Santana's eyes narrowed, and for the first time she noticed their colour, which was grey-green, and not the dark brown she had expected.

'Unfortunately for you,' he said coldly, 'I still do not consider it worth my while to continue with this meeting.'

Sharley felt her temper rise. Like two antagonists they eyed one another; the tall, slender girl and the taller, but equally slender man. Sharley wished she was wearing a trouser suit instead of a blouse and the figure-revealing skirt. In an unconscious gesture of defiance, she pushed her hair back from her face. The heavy gold bracelets on her arm jangled and the man looked at them. An indefinable expression flitted across his features and he gave what almost seemed like a half bow, yet it was so slight that Sharley was not sure whether or not she had imagined it.

'I am sorry if I seem impolite to you,' he said. 'Perhaps I may offer you a cup of coffee before you leave?'

'A drink to speed me on my way?' she commented, then nodded and preceded him into the room he indicated.

Perhaps he would thaw out over a cup of coffee and change his mind about the interview. She sat in an armchair near the fireplace. The room was warm and filled with the heavy scent of flowers, which came from a beautifully arranged vase of irises that stood on an elegant *escritoire*.

The Portuguese moved to a chair opposite her and sat down. One long, slim leg crossed over the other, and he placed his arms on either side of him, allowing his hands to rest on the sides of the chair. His hands were olive-skinned and the fingers had long, filbert-shaped nails which gleamed as if they had colourless polish on them. Sharley's eyes moved up quickly to his face, and noted with amazement that he was surveying her equally intently. His eyes ranged from her face to her feet and then up again, pausing briefly on her breasts. No, the man was certainly not effeminate, she decided, and wished he would not look at her in this particular way.

'How long are you staying in England, *senhor*?' she asked.

'Until my negotiations are completed.'

'Is the merger definitely going through?'

He said nothing, and the continuing silence told her he had no intention of answering her.

'I'm not a fool, *senhor*,' she said with some asperity. 'Sir George wouldn't have arranged for me to see you if he hadn't thought there would be a merger between his company and yours.'

'I realise that.'

'He might also be surprised if you don't let me interview you.'

'I doubt it.'

This was true, but she did not like him any the better for saying so. Before she could make any comment, the manservant wheeled in a trolley bearing a silver tray and coffee pot, with two porcelain cups. Marcos Santana spoke to him in Portuguese, his voice sounding fluid and soft in his own tongue. The servant nodded and went out, and Marcos Santana rose to pour the coffee, his hands deft, his movements well co-ordinated.

Sharley accepted a cup from him and wished there was some way to break through the aloof barrier he was successfully putting up. Did he genuinely object to being interviewed by her? It seemed hard to believe.

'I didn't realise that Portuguese men were so behind the times,' she said.

'Behind the times?' Santana looked puzzled.

'In not wishing to be interviewed by a woman.'

'Ah.' His expression cleared. 'It is merely a personal idiosyncrasy of mine, though I have no doubt that many of my compatriots would feel the same.'

'Don't you employ women in your business?'

'As secretaries and such like. But wine is my main concern, and women do not have a good palate.'

Angrily Sharley tossed her head. 'In England we have some excellent women who write on wine.'

His shoulders lifted, and she realised this was a mannerism he employed when he did not wish to argue. Slowly she sipped her coffee. It was bitter, but she was not aware of pulling a face until she saw him proffer the sugar bowl. His fingers looked very brown against the whiteness of the china, and she kept her eyes on them as she took a lump. No, the nails were not polished. Their shine came from meticulous buffing.

'Would you like me to get you some cream?' he suggested.

'I prefer it black,' she lied, not wishing to accept a favour from him.

Taking up his own cup, Santana sipped from it, then drained it completely. Sharley saw this as a sign that he wanted her to leave, but she obstinately refused to take any notice of it.

'It's excellent coffee,' she lied again. 'Do you think I might have another cup?'

The sharp look he gave her showed that she had not fooled him, but in silence he refilled her cup. She drank from it, finding this one even more bitter than the first.

'I've held my present job with the *Weekly News* for three years,' she said, 'and this is the first time anyone has refused me an interview because I'm a woman. In a way, I'm pleased it's happened, otherwise I might have believed that we were finally emancipated. At least now I know we still have something to fight for.'

'Fighters will always find something for which they can fight,' he said smoothly.

Implicit in the words was the suggestion that she was aggressive, and she had to stifle the urge to deny it. The only way to combat this man was with subtlety. But she could not think of anything subtle to say. In fact it was hard even to think. The room seemed suddenly airless, and she put her hand to her throat and felt that her skin was slightly damp. Hazily she saw Santana put his cup on the tray and then make the same gesture to the side of his face.

'It's very hot in here,' she murmured. The words came out slowly, for her tongue had difficulty in moving. 'Do you think you could open a window? I feel rather faint.'

'Perhaps it's the flowers,' he said. 'They have a very strong perfume.'

His voice seemed to come from a long way away, and as he moved to the window, Sharley tried to focus on him with all the intensity she could muster. He put his hand on the latch, then staggered and caught hold of the sill. Sharley tried to get up, but her legs would not obey her. Her limbs seemed weighted with lead and she could no longer support them. Her head lolled forward, her lids closed and oblivion took over.

CHAPTER TWO

A DULL throbbing in her head made Sharley put her hand to her temple. The movement brought her arm up against something soft and, as her fingers explored it, she realised it was a pillow. Had she just come to bed, or should she be getting up?

She was so tired she could not believe it was morning yet. She opened her eyes and saw the ceiling above her. It was pale blue, and she stared at it. Her own ceiling was white. It must be a trick of the light that had changed the colour. Slowly she lifted her head from the pillow and from the corner of her eye saw something dark on the outer edge of her vision. She turned towards it and her eyes opened wide in horror.

She was in bed with a man. Even worse, she did not know him.

Recoiling to the edge of the mattress, she went on staring at him. It was a man she had never seen before in her life. She frowned. No, that was untrue; she *had* seen him before. Memory returned and she sat up with a gasp. The sheet around her fell away and with a stifled scream she saw she was naked. Clawing up the sheet, she held it against her. Perspiration broke out all over her body and she thought she was going to faint. What was happening to her? Had she gone mad? How could she be lying naked in bed with Marcos Santana?

Another wave of heat engulfed her and she glanced quickly at the sleeping man. Like her, he also appeared to be naked, the lines of his body clearly visible beneath the softly draped sheet. Even in her highly charged state, she could not help noticing that the part of him which was uncovered was a glowing bronze in colour, the skin so smooth and glistening that it could have been satin. Surprisingly, his shoulders were wide, the muscles noticeable across his back as he lay with his body half turned. His profile could be clearly seen against the whiteness of the pillow, the nose long and straight, the lips narrow but sensually cut, a well-defined curve to the upper one. His eyelashes were long and curling as those of a girl, and she knew that this had added to his air of effeminacy when she first met him.

Involuntarily Sharley glanced at her wrist. She was still wearing her watch and she saw it was six o'clock. The full implication of the situation was now beginning to dawn on her, and she wondered if the man was mad.

First he had pretended he was not going to let her interview him. Then he had invited her to have coffee, which he had drugged in order to . . . She shook her head. No, it was impossible. If he had molested her in any way, she would know it. Or would she?

Sharley lifted the sheet and looked down at her body. To her surprise she saw she was still wearing her tights and black silk panties. Somehow she found this reassuring. She could not believe that a man who had raped her would go to the trouble of half-dressing her again afterwards.

Carefully she slid her feet out of bed and on to the carpet. Part of the sheet came with her and the movement of it made the man stir. One bronzed arm came out to catch hold of the sheet, then the long lashes fluttered and the lids lifted. For a brief second the grey-green irises were blank, then astonishment, followed by fury, filled them.

'*Dios!*' He jerked upright. The action pulled the sheet away from Sharley and his eyes widened.

Scarlet-faced, she caught at the edge of it and bunched

it up in front of her.

'I don't know what game you're playing,' she said huskily, so near to tears that she was not sure she could control them, 'but I——'

'You think *I* did this to you?'

Astonishment momentarily seemed to paralyse him. Then with an angry exclamation he leapt from the bed. Like Sharley, he too was wearing briefs.

'Please get dressed at once,' he ordered. 'It is better if we go into the sitting-room to talk.'

He disappeared from the room and quickly Sharley put on her clothes, which were piled in a heap on a chair by the dressing-table. She was disconcerted to find she was shaking with nerves, and she wondered if it was the after-effects of the drug or the shock of her predicament.

She sat down at the dressing-table and picked up a comb to tidy her hair. Only then did she realise that someone had deliberately dishevelled it to give her a wanton look. The same someone who had undressed her, no doubt. Fury with Marcos Santana made her swing round, and she almost ran into the sitting-room.

The Portuguese was already there, once more looking his indolent self in a lightweight grey suit, the jacket cut in the latest fashion, his white shirt impeccable. It was hard to believe that a short while ago they had been lying together in the same bed, half undressed.

'I now know the reason for what has happened,' he said, holding out some Polaroid snaps. 'I found these waiting for me in here.'

Sharley moved closer to him and took them from his hand. They were all of herself and this man, and showed them together in bed in a variety of abandoned, suggestive poses. The skilful way in which the sheet had been draped around them made it look as if they were both entirely naked. It also made them look as if they were making passionate love.

'Are you saying you know why this was done?' she asked huskily, dropping the snaps on to a nearby table, as if her fingers would burn if she held them any longer.

'Yes. It is because of the merger I wish to make between my company and Fawcett and Lloyd. I knew my enemies would stop at nothing to prevent it from happening, but I did not believe they would debase themselves to this extent.' The pallor of his face made his hair look black as coal. 'You must believe that I had no idea they would sink so low.'

Sharley could not bring herself to meet his eyes: her embarrassment was too great. 'But how can these pictures affect the merger?'

The ringing of the telephone cut her short and the man strode lithely across the room to answer it. He spoke to the caller in Portuguese. She could not follow what he said, but the expression on the aristocratic face told her that the news was unpleasant.

'I have the answer to your question,' he said simply, putting down the telephone and turning to her. 'Blackmail. I thought it would be.'

Sharley sank into the nearest chair, her heart beating so loudly that she could hear it.

'The call was from our photographer friend,' Marcos Santana went on bitterly. 'A Cuban revolutionary anxious to see that my workers are not exploited any longer.'

'Is he the leader of the group which is trying to take over your company?' she asked.

'I'm not sure. Until this moment I have never heard of him. The leader, as far as I know, is a man called Pedro Lopez.'

'I see.' She pointed to the photographs again. 'Are you married, *senhor*?'

'No.'

His answer surprised her, for his horror when he had found himself in bed with her had made her decide that he was. 'Well, at least you won't have to explain them away to a wife.'

'That doesn't lessen the predicament,' he said in a tone of ill-disguised irritability. 'Copies of these photographs will still be shown to Sir George Fawcett and the other directors of his company.'

Sharley could not hide her astonishment. 'For what reason?'

His irritability increased. 'Are you so amoral that you cannot comprehend that there are still people who would find this sort of behaviour—' he pointed to the photographs '—disgusting?'

With an effort Sharley restrained her temper. 'I realise that the intention is to discredit you,' she said. 'But I still can't see why your private life should be subject to the approval of Fawcett and Lloyd. After all, there's nothing disgusting in a man and woman going to bed with each other. Since neither of us is even married, I fail to see why——'

'Obviously you fail to see,' he snapped. 'But Fawcett and Lloyd are an ultra-conservative company and would not link themselves with anyone whose behaviour is not exemplary. And once these photographs are circulated among my workers in Oporto, my good reputation will be destroyed, ruined.'

Sharley stared at him, absorbing what he had said, but still not understanding it. 'You mean the men who took those photographs will show them to your workers as well?'

'Yes.'

'And they'll despise you because of it?'

'Yes,' he repeated, his face pale beneath its tan. 'Not because of what I was doing,' he said in a low voice, 'but because I had allowed myself to be seen doing it. Photographs like these suggest it was—that it ... er ... was an orgy. That other people were present who could see us.'

Sharley's own face paled, and she began to appreciate the difficulty of the situation he was in.

'What would your blackmailers have done if I hadn't come here to see you?' she asked.

'Found some other way of bringing a woman here to meet me,' he said. 'I have no doubt they would have managed it. They are clever and cunning. But your coming here was ideal for them.'

'What a mess!' Sharley felt compassionate towards him, and wished that she didn't. 'Are you sure you aren't exaggerating the position a little?'

'If only I were,' he cried passionately. 'But believe me, I am not.'

He began to pace the floor, lithe as a tiger and looking twice as dangerous. Finally he came to a stop directly in front of her, looming tall as she raised her head to stare into his eyes.

'My relationship with the men and women in my employ is quite different from anything you are used to in this country. Most of the people who work for me have inherited their jobs from their fathers and grandfathers. We are like a huge family. To them, the Santana Port Wine Company is an institution—a way of life. The name Santana has always been revered, and the men who bear that name know that their conduct must always be above reproach; that it must be an example to those they employ.'

Sharley listened intently. Marcos Santana was describing a way of life which no longer existed in England, nevertheless it was one which she could appreciate.

'Can't you explain to your employees that you were

framed?' she ventured.

'Who would believe me?'

'Everyone who knows you.'

'Few people know me,'. he replied with autocratic dignity. 'And to explain my conduct is unthinkable.'

'Well, you'd better start thinking about doing it,' she said tartly. 'You've got yourself into a tricky situation, and you're the only one who can get yourself out of it.'

'Not quite.'

She stared at him.

'Not quite,' he repeated. 'You could help me if you wish.'

Sharley let out her breath slowly. 'Well, of course, if there's anything I can do . . .'

She paused, wondering whether to tell him that Sir George Fawcett was her godfather. A quick explanation to Uncle George and Marcos Santana's good reputation in England would be preserved, leaving him only to deal with his workers in Oporto.

'I know Sir George will believe me if I tell him what happened,' she said.

'He will believe me, too,' the man replied. 'He is sufficiently intelligent to know I am not the type who would make love to . . . Who would be found in such circumstances.'

Sharley's cheeks flamed and the man looked momentarily discomfited.

'I did not mean to insult you,' he said abruptly. 'But you must appreciate that if I wished to have a love affair I would not have it with someone who could—who might——'

'Make a good story out of it with her newspaper? Your knowledge of British journalists is somewhat antiquated, *senhor*. These days, going to bed with a man is not considered important enough to merit any attention whatever—let alone blackmail or a news story!'

'Indeed? Yet your gossip columns thrive on such items.'

'Only when one of the people concerned is well known in this country.' Her look was scathing. 'And though you may be a whale in your own little pond, you're a very small fish in ours.'

White teeth gleamed in a face that was suddenly dark. 'The smallest piranha can be as deadly as the largest whale.'

Emulating him by giving a shrug, she stood up. Santana's eyes flicked over her and this time she forced herself to meet them, trying to forget that a short while ago she had been lying half naked in bed with him.

'Who organised the blackmail scheme?' she blurted out.

'My manservant.'

'What faithful retainers you have!'

'My own manservant, who normally accompanies me abroad, was taken ill with food poisoning. I see now that he was deliberately made ill, so that he could be replaced by a man who was in the pay of the Cuban. He drugged the coffee, and when we were unconscious he put us to bed and brought the photographer into the apartment.'

'What are you going to do?' Sharley asked, remembering he had said she could help him.

'There is only one thing I can do.' He bent and picked up the photographs, flicking through them with his long fingers.

'Must you look at them again?' she demanded, resisting the urge to snatch them from him.

Surprised, he lifted his head and looked at her. Her expression made him apologetic for the first time.

'Forgive me, I had not assumed you would be embarrassed by them.'

'Why should I be?' she asked sarcastically. 'I'm used to

jumping in and out of bed with every strange man I meet.'

'In Portugal,' he said drily, 'we are inclined to think this is what women in Britain and America frequently do.'

'Then the Portuguese had better revise their opinions of the outside world,' she snapped, and almost told him that until this afternoon she had never been in bed with any man. Let him think she was sexually liberated. At least that was better than being as narrow-minded and pre-judiced as he was. 'I'll leave you to deal with the photographs as you think best,' she concluded, moving to the door.

'But you promised to help me.' His anxious tone made her stop in her tracks, and he resumed speaking. 'These photographs can only harm me if they can be used to show me in a compromising situation. But if I can turn it into a situation that looks—that looks normal . . .'

'Normal?' She was puzzled. 'Even painting a nightdress over me won't do that!'

His lips tightened. 'That was not my intention. What I wish to say is that to show me in bed with a woman is one thing, but if the woman happens to be my *novia*—my fiancée, you understand—and one who will soon become my wife, then the attempted blackmail would lose all its sting.'

'You mean some Portuguese men do go to bed with their fiancées before marriage?' Sharley asked sarcastically.

'Not usually,' came the cold reply. 'But if the *novia* were not Portuguese—as you are—then it would be more likely.'

'Are you suggesting we pretend to be engaged?'

'Yes. And also that we get married.'

'You're mad!'

'Necessity makes me so. But it isn't as foolish a scheme as you think. It will work if you are willing to play your part.'

'But you don't know anything about me,' she protested.

'What's your name?' he asked casually.

'Charlotte Boswell.'

His eyebrows rose. 'So you are the aggressive woman who spoke to me on the telephone earlier today? I should have guessed.' He favoured her with another piercing look. 'Since, on your admission, you are not married, why are you unwilling to help me?'

'Because it's a crazy idea.'

'What is crazy about becoming my wife?' he questioned icily. 'Many women would consider it a great honour.'

'Not this one,' Sharley replied.

'The marriage would only be temporary, Miss Boswell, and in a register office, so that there would be no religious complications in getting it annulled.'

This was his way of making it clear how temporary he wanted it to be, and Sharley half-smiled.

'It's the only way out for both of us,' he went on. 'If you are my fiancée, then the photographs are worthless and our reputations remain intact.'

'My reputation would remain intact whether I married you or not. Luckily my friends would believe me when I told them the truth about this—this unsavoury incident. I might even be able to get my editor to print the story. In fact, I'm sure I can. We could say exactly what happened and turn the tables on the very men who are trying to discredit you.'

'It would mean a blaze of publicity,' Marcos Santana replied. 'And there is no guarantee that my workers would believe the story. They are not sophisticated people, but simple peasants who understand only one course of behaviour. A rigid one by your standards, admittedly, but it is one that has served them well.'

'You mean they wouldn't believe you'd been drugged?'

'Some of them would, and some wouldn't. But by the time Pedro Lopez has done his dirty work, he will have stirred up so much mud that Fawcett and Lloyd will refuse to go through with the merger.'

'Nor if I told Sir George the truth,' Sharley reminded him.

'Even if he believed us he would not be able to curb the scandal, and the one thing he dislikes more than anything else is publicity of this type. He will probably be next year's Lord Mayor of London and his main concern is that none of his companies should gain any notoriety. Much as he wishes for this merger, he would have no option but to break off negotiations.'

'And if he did?'

'Then my own company is doomed. The only way we can hope to resist being taken over by the militants is for us to be controlled by a large and important British company.'

'Would it be so terrible if you *were* taken over? I appreciate that from your personal point of view——'

'I am not concerned with my personal viewpoint,' he interrupted. 'I have all the money I need. But the majority of my workers do not wish for any change. Unfortunately they are ill equipped to fight the small faction who are determined to bring change about.'

'Even if you win against them now,' Sharley demanded, 'what guarantee do you have that they won't try again at a later stage?'

'By then, I hope to have started to change things myself. I have big plans for my company, Miss Boswell, but they need not concern you. Your only concern is with my present predicament. You are the only person who can save me. I give you my word it will be a marriage in name only, and that the instant we can part, we will obtain an annulment.'

'I still can't do it.'

'Why not? Don't you trust me?' All indolence gone, Santana drew himself up to his full height. 'I realise you do not wish to marry me, and I assure you the feeling is mutual. But it is my only hope.'

Sharley did not doubt that he was speaking the truth. He obviously loathed the idea of marrying her. She would not have been human if she had not felt slighted by his attitude, for she had never lacked for male admirers, many of whom would cheerfully have given up their freedom in order to marry her. But this snobbish, pretentious man actually believed he was doing her a favour. Well, not quite a favour, but he showed no embarrassment in making it clear that she would never be his own choice. He probably preferred some docile little woman who would worship at his feet—and be willing to kiss them too. She glanced down at his highly polished shoes and half smiled to herself.

'You find my situation amusing, Miss Boswell?'

'Oh no,' she said quickly. 'I was ... er ... thinking about something else.'

'Unfortunately I can't.' He sighed deeply. 'I realise I am asking for a great sacrifice on your part, but I am not pleading for myself. I think only of the thousands of men and women whose livelihood depends on the Santana Company. If the revolutionaries take over, they will ruin it within a couple of years. They will break contracts that have existed between us and other companies. They will try to find different markets and ignore the Western ones. And by the time they have learned that the West is our biggest outlet, Santana's trade will have been usurped by other companies. I am not pleading for myself,' he reiterated, 'but for those whose livelihood depends on *my* expertise.'

Sharley did not wish to be influenced by what he was saying, but she could not help it. So he was not always the cool, indolent man he appeared but, when he chose, could be deeply passionate in his sincerity.

'Wouldn't it be enough if we were just engaged?' she asked. 'Is it necessary for us to marry?'

'I am afraid so—and we would have to marry quickly. It is the surest way of making these photographs worthless.'

'Your enemies might still use them.'

'I can give you no guarantee that they won't,' he said quietly, 'though I will do everything in my power to prevent it. But even if they did use them, they would discredit themselves more than us. In Portugal one does not besmirch a man's wife without the discreditor losing honour too.'

'Then the quicker we get married the quicker we can get unmarried,' she said lightly.

'Then you agree?'

'Only because I hate to think of blackmailers winning. And also because what you said about your workers and your company makes sense to me.' Sharley hesitated. 'I— naturally I would like permission to disclose the whole story, or a great deal of it, once the whole thing is over. We wouldn't print the photographs, of course,' she said hastily, 'but we could give the lowdown on the way they tried to blackmail you.'

'Are you saying you will not agree to the marriage unless I give you that permission?' he asked.

'No, *senhor*. That would make me no better than the blackmailers. It was merely a suggestion.'

'Then I suggest we talk about it at a later date. In the meantime, with your permission, I will arrange for our marriage.'

'You won't find it easy,' she warned, knowing that the only way to avoid any embarrassment between them was to be as factual as possible about everything. 'If you were British we could get a special licence, but——'

'I will talk to my Ambassador,' he cut in. 'He is a cousin of mine.'

'I imagine you have many cousins in high places?'

'I have,' he replied, ignoring the sarcasm in her voice. 'In England you have the "old school tie". In my country we have large and helpful families.'

Sharley deliberately stopped herself from smiling at this remark. There was something about this man that made her reluctant to show him he could amuse her.

'I came here to write a story,' she said quietly. 'I never thought I would end up in it myself.'

'I regret that this afternoon has been enlightening for both of us.' The man moved ahead of her and opened the door of the sitting-room to let her precede him into the hall. 'I will go to the Embassy at once and see what can be arranged. But please do not be surprised if we are married within the next forty-eight hours.'

This time Sharley did smile. 'I don't think anything you did could surprise me, *senhor*.'

He looked at her blankly, and she had the impression he was not used to being teased. Then he gave a faint smile in return, though his eyes remained cool.

'I will call you later this evening, with your permission.'

Sharley nodded, and was at the front door when she remembered he did not have her telephone number. Quickly she scribbled it on one of her cards and gave it to him. It looked very white between his brown fingers, and they moved along its edge as though he would have liked to crush it in his hand and throw it away. She knew that much as she disliked the idea of marrying a stranger, he disliked it even more.

'Are you sure there's no other way out?' she asked.

'If I can think of one, I will let you know when I call you,' he promised earnestly. 'Until then, I bid you goodbye.'

CHAPTER THREE

It was only when she was at home, later that evening, that Sharley realised she could not keep her promise to marry Marcos Santana. She should never have allowed him to coerce her into agreeing to it and, had she not been suffering from the effects of the drugged coffee at the time, she was certain she would have put up far more resistance.

But now the drug had worn off, and she could see the drawbacks to the scheme. Not that the drawbacks alone had caused her to change her mind. Even if the plan had been watertight, she could not marry a man she did not know. The prospect of telling him this to his face was unnerving, and she decided to write him a letter, and send it to him in the morning by special messenger.

She was already at her desk, pen in hand, when the telephone rang. It was Marcos Santana.

'I tried to get you at your office,' he said without preamble, 'but you had left.'

'My hours are pretty flexible.'

'Indeed!' He dismissed her remark. 'We have been invited to have dinner with Sir George Fawcett and some of his fellow-directors. It will be an excellent opportunity for me to introduce you as my fiancée.'

'Oh no!' she exclaimed in alarm. 'There's something I want to tell you. I can't go through with the plan. I should never have agreed to it.'

'I will not allow you to back out now,' he snapped. 'You have given me your word.'

'I didn't!'

'You did. Had you not done so, I would never have told Sir George.'

'Please, *senhor*,' she said desperately. 'I can't——'

'I refuse to discuss it now. We are expected at Sir George's at eight-thirty. I will pick you up in an hour.'

The line went dead and, exasperated, Sharley put down the receiver. She was in two minds what to do. Should she wait until the Portuguese arrived and then flatly tell him she was not going to change her mind, or should she go out with him and try to persuade him that they should become engaged instead of married? Surely if she became his fiancée it would be sufficient to prevent the photographs from being published?

For the first time she considered the possibility of her godfather seeing the pictures, and her cheeks burned with shame. It was imperative that she tell him the truth about them immediately. For this reason alone, she would accept Marcos Santana's invitation for this evening.

Normally she was not a girl who gave special thought to her appearance. She had instinctive good taste and her greyhound slimness made her look elegant in the cheapest of garments. But tonight she particularly wanted to look her best, and she took several dresses from her wardrobe before finally deciding on a sophisticated black crêpe, with a severely plain bodice and long, narrow skirt. She piled her blonde hair on top of her head and took great care with her make-up, wearing more eye-shadow and mascara than usual, but no blusher on her cheeks. Perhaps the Portuguese's anger would melt when he saw her fragile pallor. If it didn't, she was in for a difficult time.

The doorbell rang sharply and Sharley hurried to answer it. A quick glance through the peephole told her who it was, and she opened the door.

She had thought Marcos Santana good-looking at their first meeting, but tonight he was magnificent in the black and white of a dinner-suit. He was like a thoroughbred stallion, she thought, glancing swiftly at the shiny black hair, the glowing bronze skin stretched tautly across high cheekbones and firm jaw, and the superb carriage that made him look even taller than he was.

If he was in any way uncomfortable in her presence he did not show it, but stood quietly waiting for her to lead him into the sitting-room. Her flat was small, but it was tastefully furnished with some good pieces which she had brought from her parents' home, and she noticed his appraising look at them, though he made no comment.

'Are you ready?' he asked politely. 'It is time we left.'

'I want to talk to you first.'

'We can talk on the way. I dislike being late.'

'And I dislike being ordered around!' she flared.

He did not answer and Sharley, fighting back her anger, picked up her wrap. Silently they went out to the car. It was silver-grey and chauffeur-driven, but Santana signalled the driver to remain where he was and opened the door for Sharley and himself. The car drew away, and only then did he speak to her.

'It is most important that we continue our engagement, Miss Boswell. A few moments after you left my apartment, I had another call from our Cuban well-wisher. He has given me twenty-four hours to hand over my business to my workers. If I refuse, the photographs will be published. That is why it is imperative for us to announce our betrothal immediately.'

'I understand your predicament, *senhor*,' she said. 'But I can't marry you. You are a complete stranger to me and——'

'It won't be a real marriage,' he interrupted. 'It will take place in a register office.'

'A civil ceremony is just as binding as a church one.'

'Not in *my* eyes,' he replied. 'I assure you that you will be free of me before the year is out, and I am prepared to make it financially worth your while.'

Sharley went scarlet. 'I'm not making difficulties in order to get money out of you. If I felt I could help you, I would do it without payment.'

'You *can* help me,' he said firmly, and leaned towards her. 'You are an intelligent young woman, and you know very well that the security and well-being of my workers are at stake. Believe me, Miss Boswell, if I give in and do as these militants want, in a year from now my company will cease to exist and my employees—who would have been secure in their jobs for the rest of their lives—will find themselves without work.'

'Are you sure you aren't exaggerating? Obviously you want to retain control of your family business, but——'

'I have nothing to gain from it personally,' he interrupted. 'Our profits go into the Santana Trust and are used to benefit the company and its employees.'

'Then why aren't the militants satisfied with *that?*'

'Because they wish to break the Trust and use all the money for their own purposes. At least the Cubans would.'

Santana angrily muttered something in Portuguese, and Sharley was sorry she did not understand what he was saying. From his expression it would have been educative.

'Please, Miss Boswell,' he said abruptly, 'think it over again, and don't make a final decision until you have met Sir George and the other directors.'

'I already know Sir George,' she said, thinking it was time she owned up to being his goddaughter.

'I know you do. It was because Sir George told me you were an excellent reporter that I agreed to let you interview me.'

'He doesn't only know me as a reporter,' she began, and was unable to continue because the car had come to a stop outside Sir George's double-fronted home on the north side of Regent's Park.

'We will talk later,' Marcos Santana said softly and, with a firm hand under her arm, guided her up the three steps to the front door.

It was opened by the butler, an elderly man who had known Sharley since she was a child, and he gave her a friendly smile before leading them across to the drawing-room.

It was filled with people, but Sir George and his wife came forward instantly to greet them. Before Sharley's escort could make the introductions, Madge Fawcett caught her close in an affectionate embrace.

'Sharley dear, what a naughty girl you are to be such a stranger! Did George tell you I'm expecting you to come down to Wiltshire for the weekend?'

'Yes, I did,' her husband interposed, and then introduced Marcos Santana to his wife.

Madge Fawcett gave the tall, suave Portuguese an admiring glance and then, as her husband drew him to one side, she enquiringly turned to Sharley.

'I was quite astonished when Senhor Santana rang George and asked if he could bring you along,' she said in a low voice. 'When did you meet him?'

'This afternoon,' Sharley murmured. 'Uncle George arranged for me to interview him.'

'What a wily old matchmaker!'

'It's nothing like that,' Sharley said hurriedly, and then stopped, thinking what a bombshell it would be if Marcos Santana suddenly announced that they were engaged to be married.

Surreptitiously she glanced at him. He was still talking to Uncle George but, as if aware of her watching him, he moved his head to look at her. Their eyes met and she tensed, almost as if he had touched some sensitive spring coiled deep within her. Quickly she told herself not to imagine things. Her reaction was the normal one of any girl who found herself in the presence of an extremely handsome man. And there was no doubt this' one was particularly good to look at, though he gave the impression of being totally oblivious of it. Was that because he was used to Portuguese females swooning over him, or was it a genuine lack of conceit?

Again Sharley was conscious of her illogical dislike of him, though she was logical enough to know she could not blame him for his different social attitudes. He came from a country whose religion, culture and heritage set it apart from the rest of the modern world.

'I'm glad you and Sharley got on so well,' Sir George remarked to Marcos, his eyes including his goddaughter in the conversation. 'I'm sure she'll do an excellent article about you.'

'I did not realise you were quite so well acquainted,' Marcos Santana replied stiffly.

'Not realised?' Sir George pretended to be astonished. 'My dear chap, an oversight on my part, I'm afraid. I thought I told you Sharley is my goddaughter?'

Grey-green eyes surveyed Sharley with a look she was beginning to know. Marcos Santana did not like to be taken unawares, and he was obviously annoyed to find he would have to change his attitude towards her. An efficient woman reporter was one thing, but an efficient woman reporter who was also the goddaughter of the illustrious chairman of Fawcett and Lloyd was quite another matter.

'There are two or three of our directors whom you still haven't met,' Sir George was speaking to the younger man again, at the same time leading him towards the other side of the room.

Sharley was left alone with Madge Fawcett, and was

immediately subjected to one of her godmother's searching looks.

'In my young days we would have described Senhor Santana as a dreamboat,' she said. 'Do you think the same?'

'Women are women,' Sharley said drily.

'I wish I was a younger one when I look at *him*.' Madge Fawcett gave a regretful sigh. 'George says he's awfully intelligent too.'

'And stubborn, dictatorial and old-fashioned,' Sharley added. 'So you see, dear aunt, even a rose has thorns.'

'You're only whetting my appetite,' came the humorous reply. 'I like a man who knows his own mind.'

Before Sharley could answer, Marcos Santana was at her side, holding out a glass of champagne for her, and her godmother beamed at them both and tactfully edged away.

Sharley made a face at the goblet he was carrying. 'Oh dear, I'm not awfully fond of champagne.'

'Shall I get you something else?'

'Yes, please. But could you make it non-alcoholic?'

He turned to a maid walking past with a tray of drinks, and then handed Sharley a glass of tonic water with lemon.

'I'm afraid it's the best I can do.'

'It doesn't matter. I shall wait until dinner. Uncle George always serves superb wine.'

'I am glad you at least appreciate *that*. For a moment I was afraid you might be a teetotaller.'

'Would it be so dreadful if I were?' she asked sweetly.

'Not dreadful. Merely a waste. There is nothing to compare with the taste and pleasure that comes from drinking a good wine.'

'Nothing? Oh, really, *senhor*, you must be joking!'

'I was talking about wine, not of other kinds of pleasure.'

She tossed her head. 'Personally, I'd as soon have a glass of milk. Preferably Jersey.'

'You will change your mind when you try my own special port. Santana Reserve is incomparable.' There was a glint in his eyes. 'Though I'm sure *you* will find something to dislike about it. You enjoy being contrary.'

Angrily she glared at him. 'You don't know me well enough to make such sweeping statements.'

'I have never found women difficult to understand.'

His conceit rendered her speechless and, because she also knew his remark was probably true, she was irritated.

'As you are such a good judge of character, *senhor*, you won't be surprised to discover I have not changed my mind about refusing to marry you. I cannot go through with it.'

'Not at any price?' He saw the flare in her eyes and immediately bit his lower lip. 'Forgive me, I had no right to say that. I realise it isn't a question of money.'

'You're quick to learn.'

'But you are intelligent,' he went on. 'Surely you appreciate the responsibility I feel towards people whose livelihood depends on me?'

'No one's livelihood has ever depended on *me*,' she informed him, 'and please don't make the mistake of thinking that my background is similar to yours or my godfather's. My mother is his cousin, but my father is a country doctor with no pretensions to grandeur.'

'But good British stock nevertheless,' the Portuguese replied, and she sighed, knowing what he meant and knowing, too, that he was right. If the livelihood of so many people depended on his continuing to run the Santana Company, she would find it difficult not to help him. Without answering him, she sipped her drink.

At dinner, Sharley was seated opposite Marcos
Santana. Whenever she glanced his way she found him
looking at her, and though she tried to avoid his gaze, she
was tinglingly aware of his presence. It was as if his eyes
were touching her skin, setting it on fire with the barely
controlled temper that smouldered in them.

Considering he wanted to enlist her aid, she thought
mutinously, he was not going the right way to get it. Any
other man would have exerted all the charm he possessed
in order to sway her. But this one merely looked down his
aristocratic nose at her and took it for granted she would
bow to his wishes.

Yet surprisingly, the more Sharley thought about his
attitude, the more her anger ebbed. It was amusing, in
fact, to meet a man as chauvinistic as this one. Obviously
the ladies in Portugal had a totally different outlook from
British ones, and it might be fun to try to cut this particular male down to size.

As the meal progressed, the conversation became live-
lier, and Marcos Santana held his own very well. He was
able to converse with a fluency that surprised Sharley, on
a diversity of subjects. He might be narrow-minded where
women were concerned, but on social and political topics
he was worldly-wise.

After dinner, the women retired, leaving the men alone
with their port and brandy. Sharley was sure the men
would start to talk about business and when, after half an
hour in the drawing-room with middle-aged female chatter boring her to death, there was still no sign of anyone
emerging from the other side of the hall, she gave her
godmother a look of entreaty.

Madge Fawcett glanced at her wrist-watch with a
frown. 'I'll lay a wager that no one will come out of the
dining room until it's time for everyone to go home. Next
time this happens, I'm going to take all the ladies to a

gambling casino. That'll blow the profits.'

'Don't fret,' one of the other wives chided. 'It's much more restful for us to be alone like this.'

'At least we can put our feet up comfortably,' the wife of another director smiled, and surveyed Sharley thoughtfully. 'I expect you and Senhor Santana will go on to a disco when you leave here?'

Sharley tried unsuccessfully to see Marcos Santana letting himself go in a disco. It was as difficult as trying to imagine herself in his arms. She blushed vividly and lowered her eyes as she recalled the intimate poses in the photographs. What had he done with them? She did not relish the prospect of his looking at them again. Glancing at her godmother, she saw speculative amusement on her face.

'You're blushing, Sharley.'

'I think I had too much wine at dinner,' Sharley lied, and turned quickly as the door opened. It was the butler.

'Sir George would like to see you in the library, Miss Boswell,' he said.

Aware of the other women's surprise, Sharley went swiftly from the room. Had Marcos already told Uncle George of their engagement? If he had, then her godfather would surely realise it was a pretence. No one who knew her well could believe she and the Portuguese were in love. She opened the library door and saw that her godfather was alone.

'Come in, my dear,' he said quietly. 'I want to talk to you.'

'Senhor Santana has told you everything?' she asked, knowing full well that he had.

'Yes.' Her godfather waited until she was seated opposite to him before he continued. 'It's important that our merger with the Santana Company goes through. Not only because of the financial conditions, but because of the political implications.'

'Political?'

'Yes, my dear. The Santana Company is not only concerned with port wine, but has close associations with
other industries throughout Portugal. It's because of this
that the Portuguese government doesn't want it to be
taken over by the militant group who are trying to oust
Marcos. If these men succeed, then a gang of highly dangerous people will gain a foothold in Portuguese industry.'

'Then surely it's up to the government to step in? Why
let Senhor Santana fight them alone?'

'Because the government don't want to disclose their
hand. They're treading a narrow diplomatic path, and
one slip could be fatal. But I assure you they're behind
Marcos in every way. And so am I. That's why I want
you to help him.'

Sharley avoided Sir George's eyes. 'I assume you've
seen the photographs?'

'Yes,' he sighed. 'It places Marcos in an unpleasant
situation, and we must help him to deal with it. I'm extremely sorry that you're implicated, and I appreciate
that it must be abhorrent for you to marry someone under
such circumstances. But I can't see any other way out.'

'But marriage is so final,' she exclaimed.

'It will only be a business arrangement,' her godfather
stated. 'It needn't be for longer than six months. Then
you can have it annulled.'

'Isn't there any other way out of the situation? I know
I agreed to it earlier today, but when I thought about it
afterwards, it seemed such an extreme step to take.'

'Try not to think of it as a real marriage,' Sir George
reiterated, and then gave a faint smile. 'This is an odd
conversation for the two of us to be having. I anticipated
that *I* would be the old-fashioned one.'

'And that I'd be the liberated female who'd look on marriage as unimportant?'

'I should have known better,' Sir George said. 'After all, you are the product of your upbringing, rather than your present environment.'

'I'm not sure Senhor Santana thinks the same,' Sharley said drily. 'He has some very old-fashioned attitudes about working women.'

'He tends to sound more prejudiced than he is.' Sir George leaned closer. 'Will you stand by your original promise, Sharley? If you agree, I'll do everything I can to smooth things for you when the time comes for the marriage to end.'

Sharley knew he would, and some of her panic at being tied to a stranger evaporated.

'Very well,' she said slowly. 'Though I dread to think what Mother and Dad will say.'

'Leave them to me. I'll put them in the picture.'

'Would you?' she said gratefully. 'They'll be far more likely to believe *you* than me. If I told them the whole story, they'd swear I was making it up.'

'I can see why,' Sir George said ruefully. 'It *does* sound a bit like a John le Carré novel.' He paused, as if having a doubt, then pushed it away. 'I suggest we call Marcos in and tell him of your decision. He'll be delighted that you've changed your mind again.'

If Marcos Santana was relieved, he did not show it. To Sharley's chagrin he merely inclined his head when Sir George told him, almost as if he had known all along that no female could withstand his wishes for long.

'And now I suggest we join the others and tell them the news,' Sir George said.

'Please don't,' Sharley begged, suddenly horrified by the prospect.

'I wasn't suggesting we tell them the *true* reason for the

engagement,' her godfather protested. 'Merely that you and Marcos are—are in love and are going to be married.'

'I'd still rather you didn't.'

'We cannot keep it a secret for long,' Marcos Santana interposed levelly. 'The whole purpose of the marriage is for it to receive publicity.'

'Publicity can wait until tomorrow,' she rejoined.

The two men glanced at each other and Sharley, intercepting the look, knew they thought she was being irrational. But to her surprise, the Portuguese gave the faintest of smiles and nodded.

'Very well, Miss Boswell, I shall respect your wishes. I had not realised you were so shy and modest.'

'Modest about what?'

'Your good fortune in capturing me.'

'Why . . .'

Sharley's exclamation was drowned by her godfather's chuckle as he led the way back to the drawing-room.

An hour later, when Marcos was driving Sharley home, having dismissed the chauffeur, he told her that their wedding was already arranged.

'Sir George will be announcing our engagement at a reception at noon tomorrow. He thought it the best way of letting the Press know.'

'I think you might have given my newspaper the scoop,' she said drily.

'What we are doing is too important for us to think in terms of scoops,' Marcos said slowly. 'This is no game for me.'

'But it is for me,' she reminded him. 'A "let's pretend" game that I'm not very happy at playing. But I won't go back on my word,' she assured him, seeing a frown darken his face. 'Though naturally, the quicker it's all over the better.'

'I will send a car for you tomorrow at eleven-thirty,' he said, as they reached her house. 'The reception is in Sir George's office.'

'I can make my own way there.'

'Such independence is unseemly,' he said in a stiff voice. 'It is a man's duty to ensure that his fiancée arrives safely at the engagement party.'

'You worry too much about protocol, *senhor*.'

'It is also more fitting that you call me "Marcos", and I will have to call you——' he hesitated. 'Is your proper name Charlotte?'

Sharley suppressed a smile at his formality. 'That's what I was christened. But everyone calls me Sharley.'

'It is too masculine a name.'

'You're thinking of Charlie. But it's unimportant what you call me,' she added, putting the key into the lock of the door.

'I shall see you tomorrow,' he replied.

His goodnight was soft, and she knew he did not move away until she had closed the door safely behind her. Even when she heard his car drive away, he remained in her thoughts, infiltrating her dreams and making her restless and apprehensive.

At noon next day, Sharley found herself standing beside Marcos Santana in a room on the top floor of the huge building that housed Fawcett and Lloyd. Dozens of members of the national Press were present, indicating to her how important the merger was considered to be. Not only would it stabilise the Santana Company, but also, if what her godfather said was true, the Portuguese government and, with it, the many British interests in Portugal.

Thinking about the long period of friendship between the two countries, and the trade which had resulted from it, Sharley wondered why Marcos Santana should still be like an alien. His entire outlook was so different from hers that it was hard to believe they lived on the same planet, and in the same era.

Today he looked only a little less austere than the night before. He wore a dark business suit and his linen was was as impeccable as ever. His black hair was neatly brushed back from his high forehead, and gleamed like satin. A slight smile curved the corners of his mouth and he appeared to be completely at his ease. But Sharley knew better. She could sense the anger in him, and knew it could not be easy for a man of his disposition to act the happy fiancé of a girl who, under normal circumstances, he would never have noticed, let alone married.

She had no need to wonder where his personal choice lay, convinced his preference was for a curvaceous but docile girl of his own nationality and background, who would regard him as her master. Yet here he was, with one languid hand resting lightly on the arm of a slim Scottish girl, with narrow bones and blonde hair. A girl who looked more like a graceful colt than a dark-eyed dove. And to add insult to injury, she was a liberated young woman, and a journalist to boot.

Amusement curved her mouth and brought little laughter lines to the sides of her wide-apart eyes. She looked down and saw the huge blue-white diamond glittering on the third finger of her left hand. It was a beautiful ring, unsoftened by ornamentation and obviously worth a fortune, but ice-cold, which, she felt, aptly suited it to the reason for their marriage. Their union certainly had nothing to do with love.

'We shall be married by this time tomorrow,' Marcos Santana broke into her thoughts. 'My Ambassador and Sir George were able to cut through the red tape and make all the arrangements.'

'Good.' Her voice was thin. 'The sooner it's over, the sooner we can forget it.'

'I am enjoying this as little as you,' he replied icily. 'Please remember it.'

It was three o'clock before Sharley was finally able to return to her office, disappointing Aunt Madge, who had anticipated a leisurely gossip. But there were several stories requiring her attention, and she was busy sorting through them when the news editor called her in to see him.

'What's this I hear about you and Marcos Santana becoming engaged?' he demanded. 'Is Jake having me on?'

Jake was assigned to the City News desk, and had been one of the men present at the reception.

'He's telling the truth,' she admitted.

'Then why the hell did you keep it a secret? We could have printed the news yesterday, ahead of the other papers.'

'Marcos wouldn't let me.' It was surprising how easily his first name came to her lips.

'Marcos wouldn't . . .' The news editor swallowed his chagrin. 'When are you getting married—if that isn't a secret too? And how about arranging an interview with Santana for us?'

'What do you want to ask him?'

'Details of his merger with Fawcett and Lloyd.'

'He won't talk about that to anyone.'

'We aren't "anyone". We're the paper his wife works for. If you won't do it for me, Sharley, the editor will ask you to do it for *him*.'

'I'll wait until he does,' she said. 'I'm not being difficult, but I know Marcos won't talk until all his plans are completed. When he's ready, I'll see if I can get you an exclusive. Or at least try to persuade him to talk to us first.'

It was, she thought as she resumed her work, the very least Marcos should do for her. She tried not to think of all she would be doing for him, and was surprised how apprehensive she felt at their impending marriage.

She had not reached the age of twenty-three without falling in love, but each time the emotion had been fleeting. She had to respect a man in order to want him; had to feel he was intelligent and capable; yet at the same time he must not make her feel inadequate.

'You're looking for the impossible,' her mother had once said in exasperation, when she had tried to explain why she had turned down an extremely eligible young accountant.

'No, I'm not,' she had told her mother. 'I'm just looking for someone like Dad.'

Her father, hearing this, had laughed. 'You may have to compromise, Sharley. I'm a one-off.'

'Then I'll remain a spinster.'

'I doubt that. One day you'll meet someone who'll knock away all your preconceived ideas, and you'll be only too happy to bask at his feet.'

At the time Sharley had doubted it, but since meeting Marcos Santana she could see what her father meant. The Portuguese had an air of command that added to his physical attraction and, though she was immune to it, she could understand why many women would not be the same.

She twisted the diamond ring on her finger. Soon a gold one would lie next to it. Or would it be platinum; as cold and white and lifeless as their vows?

Sharley thought of this the next day as she and Marcos stood in front of the registrar. Then Marcos slipped a narrow platinum band signifying eternity on to her finger. She concentrated on the fact that in this instance eternity only meant six months at the most, yet she could not prevent the nervous trembling that swept over her as she signed her name on the marriage register. The pen slipped from her fingers and Marcos caught it. Marcos Santana, her husband. Her trembling increased as he silently wrote his name next to hers.

After the ceremony, Sir George and his wife hurried forward to embrace them, keeping up the pretence that this was a normal, happy occasion.

As they emerged from the register office, they were met by a barrage of Press photographers, and Sharley guessed her godfather had deliberately arranged it. He was leaving nothing to chance. The Portuguese newspapers would publish the pictures next morning, thereby ensuring that the marriage between Marcos Santana of the Santana Company, and the goddaughter of the chairman of Fawcett and Lloyd, received maximum publicity. So far, the schemes of Marcos' enemies had been foiled, but Sharley had a premonition that there were still dangerous times ahead.

'I had hoped to return to Portugal today,' Marcos said as they drove off in the direction of Sir George's house for the wedding luncheon, 'but I'm afraid it won't be possible for us to go until tomorrow.'

'Us?' Sharley echoed.

'Of course. I have spoken to my mother and explained the situation, but she will not be at rest until she has met you.' Marcos gave the faintest of smiles. 'She has as many doubts about the marriage as you have.'

Sharley was not interested in the way his mother was feeling. All she was concerned with was her own present position.

'Are you telling me you want me to go with you to Portugal?'

'But naturally. Where else should a bride be, if not by her husband's side?'

Sharley looked at him aghast. Not for a moment had it dawned on her that she would be expected to leave

England. She had not thought beyond the wedding ceremony and, now that she did, the full implication of the
situation appalled her.

'How long will I have—do you expect me to stay there?'
she asked.

'Long enough to give credence to the marriage, and
also until the merger with Fawcett and Lloyd is so well
established that it is an accepted fact.'

'But what about my job? I can't just walk out of it!'

Marcos looked at her in exasperation. 'You surely
didn't expect me to go to Portugal alone? Even the most
emancipated of women would not have assumed such a
thing.'

Sharley blushed. What he said made sense. How could
they maintain the pretence of being newlyweds if she
stayed in London while he lived in Oporto?

'I did not anticipate it would be such a shock for you,'
he went on. 'You surprise me very much.'

'Why?'

'Because I assumed you took the normal—er—details
of marriage for granted.'

'Of course I do,' she said indignantly. 'But ours isn't a
normal marriage, and I didn't look beyond the ceremony.'

They reached Sir George's house and Sharley asked
the question uppermost in her mind.

'What about today, then? If we're staying in London
overnight, do you expect me to move into your apartment?'

'Without question,' he answered, not looking at her.
'Please do not be worried by it. I have given you my
word that our marriage will be platonic, and——'

'I'm not frightened that you'll break your promise,' she
intervened, and stepped smartly out of the car and up the
three steps to the front door. Marcos came behind her,

looming so tall that she could see his shadow across the lintel.

'Things will not be as difficult as you think,' he said quietly. 'Please try to smile, Charlotte.'

It was the first time he had spoken her name, and he gave the last half of it a decidedly foreign drawl. She half turned to face him, and saw that his features were relaxed and less stern, as if he already felt that the threat to his company was receding.

'Once we feel less strange with each other,' he went on, 'I am sure you will enjoy your stay in my country. The weather is good and the people are friendly.'

'Not all of them.'

'Even the rebels have much to commend them,' he said surprisingly. 'They are sincere in their beliefs, which is more than one can say of many people. I am not speaking of the anarchist who arranged for those photographs to be taken, and if I ever get my hands on him . . .' Marcos stopped abruptly, as if afraid that to continue the conversation would make him lose his equilibrium. 'But let us not talk of the unhappy events that have brought us together. There will be time for that when we are in Portugal. For the moment we must play the role of bride and groom.'

'Even in the privacy of Uncle George's home?'

'There are always servants about,' came the answer, 'and it is as well to be on our guard. The man we've outwitted is no fool. He realises our marriage is an expedient one, and we must be careful not to give him a chance to expose us.'

Accepting the truth of this, Sharley braced herself to face the wedding luncheon. When it was over, she would have to return to her office to talk to Sam Morris, before going home to pack. She must also speak to her parents. Uncle George had driven down to see them, to explain the real reason for her precipitate marriage, and she had immediately received a tearful telephone call from her mother, who had needed reassurance from Sharley that she knew what she was doing.

But all at once Sharley was no longer sure. If she had known that marriage to Marcos would mean living in Portugal, it would have taken more than her godfather's pleas to persuade her to go through with it. If only she could turn back the clock!

The door opened and the butler beamed at her. 'Congratulations, Miss Bos—madam,' he corrected himself. 'And may I give you the best wishes of all the staff.'

'Thank you, Dickson,' she smiled back, and placing her slender hand on Marcos' arm, she walked into the hall.

The charade was beginning, and she must play her part to the end.

CHAPTER FOUR

THE plane banked steeply and the land below appeared to shift and turn sideways. Then the aircraft levelled out and slowly began its descent towards Pedras Rubras Airport.

The flight from London to Oporto had been smooth and, because her companion had been so silent, Sharley had found the journey boring. After making sure she was comfortable, Marcos had given all his attention to some documents in his briefcase. In a way she found it a relief, for she was still ill at ease with him. It was unusual for her to feel like this with a man, and she knew it was partly because of the unusual circumstances which had brought them together, and partly because he was so unlike any other man she had met.

Her first impression that he was effete had soon changed. His slow soft voice was merely a mask to cover a mind as quick as a fencer's lance, while his languid way of moving hid a physical co-ordination that would have done justice to an Olympic sportsman. Beneath his cool manner lay a passionate intensity of purpose, and she could not help wondering whether this also extended to his emotional life. Hurriedly she drew away from the thought. The less she knew of his emotional life the better. Mischievous fate had brought them together, but their association was only going to be a short, temporary one; within a matter of months they would go their own separate ways. Sustained by this knowledge, she settled back in her seat and closed her eyes.

'I hope you get a few good articles out of all this,' her editor had said yesterday, when she had seen him pri-

vately to tell him the whole story. 'But don't expect to be
paid while you're out of the country. In fact, I can't even
guarantee we'll be able to take you back.'

Sharley had disregarded this as being so much hot air.
She knew Sam Morris liked her work and was sure she would
be reinstated on her return. Besides, all she needed was to
publish the reason for her marriage to Marcos Santana
and the whole of Fleet Street would be clamouring for
her. With her editor's farewell ringing in her ears she had
returned to her flat, packed her clothes, and driven to
Marcos' apartment in the car he had put at her disposal.

She was not looking forward to the evening ahead of
her. It was the first time she and Marcos would be alone
for any length of time, and she hoped they would find
something to talk about that would not rouse either of
them to anger.

In the event, the next few hours were a pleasure, and
Sharley saw a side to Marcos Santana which she had not
suspected. He took her to dinner at Le Gavroche, which
served some of the best French food in London at the
most expensive prices. It was rare to obtain a table without booking a week in advance and she was curious to
know if he had intended to take someone else here. It was
strange to think of him having another life apart from his
business one, but a man who looked the way he did would
have to fight off the women. Sensual, handsome, rich and
controlled. What female could resist such a combination?
He was a fortress of masculinity that was a challenge to
be conquered.

For the first half of the meal he kept the conversation
upon light subjects: music, the books they read, the countries they had visited—all the world on his part, it
seemed—and only France and Italy on hers. Then he
started to tell her about his family estate outside Oporto,
which was considered to be one of the showplaces of the

area, and his voice was no longer light, but full of emotion.

'Our family have owned it since the middle of the seventeenth century,' he explained. 'Over the years we have acquired more and more land, although it was not until the Methuen Treaty in 1703 that we began to make any money out of port wine.'

'Why was that?'

'Because until then the import taxes into England had crippled the business.'

'What about the crippling taxes of today?'

'We still receive certain concessions. But England is no longer our biggest customer, and we have built up excellent trade with North and South America.'

Sharley nodded. 'I was forgetting Portugal used to own Brazil.'

'And much more,' he added. 'Though today we consider we are lucky to own ourselves.' He saw her puzzled expression. 'During our recent revolution we nearly lost our freedom.'

'What sort of freedom did you have under Salazar? He was a dictator, wasn't he? Or was it different for you, because of your money and position?'

'A little different, but even so I am glad that the dictatorship is at an end. I think——'

Abruptly he stopped talking, and she knew it was useless to pursue the subject. Secrecy was apparent in the heavy lids that masked his eyes, and gave his face such a brooding foreign quality.

She noticed that he smiled rarely, but when the head waiter came over to ask if they had enjoyed their meal, he gave him a smile of such warmth that he appeared almost boyish. So this lofty sprig on the noble Santana tree *did* have charm when he cared to use it; potent charm too, Sharley was sure. She must remember it in case he tried

to exert it on her. If it suited him he would try to persuade
her to stay in Portugal for longer than six months, and
she realised that the longer she remained with him, the
more dangerous it could be for her peace of mind.

The thump of aircraft wheels on the runway told her
they had landed, and she sat up instantly. But Marcos
remained motionless, still looking down at his papers, and
only when the aircraft came to a final halt did he undo
his seat-belt and rise.

With surprising ease they went through Customs clear-
ance, though Sharley's passport came in for careful scru-
tiny when it was realised she was now Portuguese by
marriage, though still a British citizen.

But they were soon speeding down a well-built highway
in a white Mercedes sports car which had been waiting
for them at the airport. Marcos drove it himself, and she
guessed he had left it parked there before coming to
England. She hid a wry smile. He could never have envisaged himself returning to it in the space of a week with
a wife by his side.

Nervously she looked at the scenery. The land immediately around them was flat, though in the near distance it rolled gently upwards. It seemed more verdant
than the English countryside, with a lushness that came
from winter rains and strong sunshine.

'Do you come to Oporto often?' she asked.

'At certain times of the year more than others. I tend
to travel in the winter, but in the summer—when the
days are long and sunny—I prefer to remain in the
country.'

She had not thought of him as an out-of-doors type,
but did not comment on it.

'Do you have much of a social life in the country?' she
went on.

'Yes. But it's entirely different from the kind you lead

in Britain. Our estates are very large and some of our neighbours live many miles away from us. Because of that, we frequently have guests staying at the *quinta* for the weekend.'

'The *quinta?*' Sharley echoed. 'Is that Portuguese for country house?'

'For a *large* country house,' he explained.

She digested this information, then sought for more.

'Do you have a large staff?'

'Enough,' he replied laconically, and aware from his tone that he did not want to discuss it further, Sharley turned to look through the window.

Trees, chestnuts, pines and elms abounded, though as the car ate up the miles these soon gave way to cultivated vineyards with long, straight rows of vines stretching as far as the eye could see.

Their arrival at Marcos' home was far more sudden that she had anticipated. She had assumed a slow approach down a long, discreet drive to some grand mansion, but they drove instead along a narrow road surrounded by vineyards and then turned sharply right to come face to face with a low-lying house. Because it was only two storeys high, it had not been visible from a distance. It was rambling and L-shaped, and built of old grey stone. There were a large number of windows and archways, and a verandah—dotted with chairs, tables and hammocks—ran along one side. Above the huge front door she noticed a coat of arms and guessed it to be the heraldic emblem of the Santana family.

As Marcos helped her out of the car, he noticed her trying to make out the inscription.

'*To the faithful, faith comes,*' he translated. 'All Santanas believe that.'

'I wish *I* did. Right now, I have no faith in anything.'

'You are thinking of people,' he said softly, 'but I was

thinking of oneself and one's relationship to God.'

Sharley could not think of anything to say to this, and he gave her a sudden smile and lightly touched her arm, almost as if to reassure her.

'Come,' he said, 'my mother is waiting.'

He led her across the verandah and into the hall. It was large and sombre, with heavy wood-panelling and a tiled wooden floor, highly polished yet not slippery underfoot. Some beautiful rugs were scattered on its surface, as well as several pieces of exquisitely carved wooden furniture; a large table, a chest of drawers and four high-backed chairs.

Sharley had no chance to take in any more, for a middle-aged woman was coming towards them. She had the same grey-green eyes and beautifully shaped thin mouth as Marcos, but since she was in no way like the Portuguese aristocrat Sharley had been expecting to meet, she was puzzled.

'Marcos, my dear, it's good to have you home again!'

The woman's words were addressed to the man, but the eyes were on Sharley, who was now totally confused, for she spoke English without a trace of an accent—except for a faint Scottish burr.

'And you must be Charlotte,' the woman went on, taking Sharley's hand in a firm clasp. 'You look tired and faintly bemused, which is the way women generally look in my son's presence.' She gave Marcos a laughing glance, which he received goodhumouredly.

'You are not to undermine my authority with my wife,' he drawled. 'As it is, I am having difficulty maintaining it.'

'All to the good if you don't.' The woman linked her arm through Sharley's. 'I will show you to your room, my dear. Or would you prefer to have a cup of tea first?'

'I'd rather have a wash before tea, if I may.'

Marcos spoke softly to his mother in Portuguese, and then turned to Sharley. 'I was making sure the master suite had been prepared for us,' he said.

Sharley was startled. 'But I'm not——'

'You are my wife,' he interposed quickly. 'It would be as well if you remembered that.'

'Surely not when we're alone in our home?'

'Even then. Walls have ears, and for the next few months we must maintain the charade.' He looked at his mother. 'I will take Charlotte to our suite myself. It is not good for you to climb up and down the stairs.'

'One flight won't harm me,' his mother said, but did as he enjoined.

Sharley followed Marcos to the first floor. Here the panelling gave way to whitewashed walls, marked every two yards by wrought-iron wall sconces. There were no rugs on the polished floor and all the doors were of heavily carved blockwood. Halfway down, Marcos stopped and indicated Sharley to precede him into an ornately-furnished sitting-room which led into an equally elaborate bedroom. Here, too, the furniture was of dark carved wood, with gold-embossed brocade at the long windows and over the enormous bed. It was a sombre room, made more so by the heavy carved ceiling.

'There's no shortage of wood here,' she commented.

'You will get used to it,' he replied.

Sharley wandered over to look into the bathroom, which she saw with relief was modern. When she stepped back into the bedroom, Marcos had gone through to the sitting-room and she joined him there.

'My own bedroom is on the other side,' he said, pointing to a door so skilfully cut into the wall that it was almost unnoticeable. 'There is a key that you can turn if it will make you feel more secure, but you need have no fear that I will bother you.'

'I'm not worried,' she said lightly.

'Good.' His face was expressionless. 'I suggest you come downstairs when you are ready.'

'I may as well unpack.'

'You may leave that for one of the maids to do.'

Sharley glanced at her watch. It was four o'clock. 'What time do you dine?'

'At eight. We keep early hours in the country because I like to rise at seven. But there is no reason for you to get up at that time. You may breakfast in your room if you wish.' He regarded her gravely. 'I hope you will look upon your stay here as a holiday. If there is anything you want which you do not already have, please tell me. I have perhaps not made it clear to you how grateful I am that you have co-operated with me.'

'I didn't have any alternative,' she remarked, and noticed wryly that her comment did not embarrass him. But she had the feeling that little would. He was a man too used to getting his own way.

'Nonetheless I am deeply appreciative of your help,' he repeated. 'So do not hesitate to tell me if there is anything you require.'

Sharley nodded and turned towards her bedroom, then stopped on the threshold. 'Do you change into formal clothes for dinner?'

'My mother does, but you may wear whatever you wish.'

'Not jeans, though?' she smiled. 'I can't see *you* wearing them.'

'I don't,' he agreed. 'But I doubt if that will deter you.' It was the first faintly humorous remark he had made, although she assumed he had meant it to be sarcastic.

'I find jeans comfortable,' she replied, and was glad she had brought a pair with her. No doubt he preferred his women to be demure and servile, in flowing skirts, but she had no intention of pandering to him. He would have to remember that she was his wife in name only. In every other respect she was free to be herself.

Alone in her bedroom, she was overcome by a wave of homesickness. The heavy atmosphere of the furnishings and the strange view from her window added to her feeling of being in an alien land.

Immediately below was a flower-filled garden ablaze with early June roses and a mass of variegated green shrubs, but beyond the shrubs lay the vineyards: acre after acre of them stretching as far as she could see, and climbing slowly but gently upwards, their green paling into grey in the distance, until they merged into the sky.

Afraid of becoming tearful if she remained alone too long, Sharley had a quick wash, combed her hair and went downstairs. She was not sure where the drawing-room was, but luckily there were no doors separating the main reception rooms, and she headed for the one which seemed to have the most settees, and found Marcos' mother seated in a corner of a satin brocaded one. In front of her was a trolley, set with a magnificent silver tea service, which included a small kettle perched atop a spirit stand.

'I'm glad you came down before Marcos,' the woman smiled. 'Now we can have a chat.'

Sharley wished she had anticipated this and remained in her room longer.

'Don't look so apprehensive, child,' the older woman smiled, deducing what Sharley was thinking. 'Marcos has told me the whole story, but I wanted to hear your side of it too. I'm very impressed by the way you agreed to help him. It shows great kindness.'

'He didn't give me much choice,' Sharley said frankly. 'Sir George also happens to be my godfather, and he put pressure on me too.'

'I can well believe that. He's partly Scottish, isn't he?'

Sharley smiled. 'Yes, he is. But that doesn't make him more obstinate than most successful company chairmen.'

'Indeed it does. We Scots are a stubborn breed. Although I've lived here since my marriage thirty-three years ago, I'm no more easily swayed than I was when I came here.'

'Thirty-three years?' Sharley questioned.

'Yes. My son is thirty-one.'

Sharley was astonished. Marcos seemed considerably older. But that was probably because he was so aloof in his manner.

'How old are *you*?' Senhora Santana asked. 'Do tell me all about yourself. Marcos merely said he met you when you went to interview him.'

Briefly Sharley recounted the story of her life, sensing that the woman was pleased by the fact that her father was a professional man and that Sir George was related to her mother.

'I always thought it very exciting the way I met *my* husband,' Senhora Santana commented, as the silver kettle came to the boil. 'This is one thing the servants have never learned to make satisfactorily for me,' she said in an aside, as she ladled tea from a caddy into the silver pot. 'My husband bought me this tea-set for our first wedding anniversary and I've used it ever since. I always hoped that one day I would give it to my daughter-in-law.' The grey-green eyes twinkled. 'Which means I've always secretly hoped that Marcos would marry a British girl. And now he has.'

'Opportunely, but not by design,' Sharley felt obliged to say.

'I know that.' The woman settled back to wait for the tea to brew. 'Help yourself to a sandwich, child. I'm sure you can't be on a diet.'

'I'm not.' Sharley heaped some wafer-thin sandwiches

on to a plate and sat down. She had not eaten since breakfast, having found it difficult to enjoy her lunch on the plane with Marcos sitting so close to her. She somehow felt she would never get used to his presence. It was amazing that a man who never raised his voice and moved in the most languorous manner should exude such an aura of authority.

'I warned Marcos that Lopez and his friends were unscrupulous enough to do anything to discredit him among his workers,' his mother said suddenly. 'But he was always convinced he could outwit them.'

'No decent person could have expected them to behave in quite such a despicable way,' Sharley replied.

'That's true—and especially so of Marcos. My son is more than decent. He's the most highly principled person I've ever known. More so even than his father.' A faint sigh accompanied these words. 'My husband would have dealt far more severely with Lopez than Marcos did. If Marcos had thrown him out the first time he made his demands—if he had refused to have any discussion with him—perhaps none of this would have happened.'

Sharley did not understand what the woman meant. 'Do you mean Pedro Lopez came here?'

'Many times. And Marcos had several meetings with him in Oporto. He told Lopez he was willing to give the workers a share in the company, and turn it into something similar to a co-operative. But whatever concession he made, Lopez always came back and demanded more. Nothing seemed to satisfy him, and his demands became increasingly impossible to meet. We realise now, of course, that Alvarez was behind it all.'

'Alvarez?'

'He's a Cuban, and the man responsible for the photographs which were taken of you and Marcos. We believe him to be the guiding force behind Lopez and the other workers. He doesn't want any agreement to be reached. His plan is to break up the company regardless of the consequences. People like Alvarez aren't really on the side of the men they're professing to help. They're anarchists with an inbuilt desire to create discord.'

'I hadn't realised your son had ever negotiated with Lopez,' said Sharley, still reflecting on the earlier part of the conversation, and wondering if her godfather knew about it.

'Marcos never mentions it. He's become so incensed by their behaviour and the way they rejected every one of his schemes that he's turned completely against them. It's made him far more intransigent than I've ever known him to be.' The woman poured the tea. 'All his life he's been a gentle and considerate person. Good behaviour and consideration for others come naturally to him, and his main concern has always been the welfare of those who work for him. But months of negotiations with Lopez—Alvarez has always stayed hidden in the back-ground—has made him go to the other extreme. Now he can see no good in *any* of Lopez' suggestions.'

'I don't think I could either,' Sharley said emphatically. 'His behaviour is beyond description.'

'Not *his* behaviour,' Senhora Santana insisted. 'He only did what Alvarez ordered him to do.'

'That still makes him equally responsible.'

There was a pause before Senhora Santana sighed and nodded. 'I suppose you're right, but please don't tell Marcos. I still hope I can influence him to change his mind.'

'Change his mind about what?'

'About the impending merger with Fawcett and Lloyd. I don't believe that the way it's been organised at the moment will work in the long term. I think Marcos' original intention of forming a workers' co-operative was the right way, and it could still be done with Sir George's co-operation.'

'I thought your government didn't want a co-operative?'

'They don't want the kind that Alvarez has in mind. But they aren't against the one which Marcos originally proposed. My belief is that in a matter of five or ten years, private companies will cease to exist in this country. That's why it's so important for Marcos to come to a compromise while he can still do so.'

Sharley could not help but agree with this far-sighted view, and it was obvious, from the way Marcos had originally tried to negotiate with Pedro Lopez, that he thought so too.

'I hope you will help me to influence my son,' Senhora Santana said firmly.

'I don't have any influence with him,' Sharley replied. 'I barely know him.'

'You're his wife. Although it was a marriage of necessity, he will still, subconsciously, defer to you in many things. All I ask is for you to use that influence to help me. With persuasion, one can do a great deal with Marcos—as I was able to do with my own husband.'

'We can't compare our marriages,' Sharley said stubbornly. 'Your son and I don't love each other.'

'I know, my dear. But he owes you a great deal. For this reason alone, he may heed your advice.'

'I wouldn't be too sure, Mrs Santana.' Sharley paused. 'Or should I call you Senhora?'

'I would prefer you to call me Dona Ana.'

'Ana doesn't sound very Scottish,' Sharley commented.

'My full name is Fiona Anne,' came the smiling answer. 'But my husband found Fiona too hard to pronounce.'

Sharley grinned, wondering whether it was a habit of the Santana men to change their wives' names.

The old woman looked questioningly at the expression on her face. 'Does that amuse you?'

'Yes, because it's quite the reverse with Marcos. He's taken my name—which is an easy one—and turned it into something longer and more difficult. He calls me Charlotte because he thinks Sharley too masculine.'

'Trust Marcos!' Dona Ana laughed.

Sipping her tea, Sharley mused that trusting Marcos was not something she could yet do completely. But she did not feel quite as desolate as when she had first arrived here. It was probably because her mother-in-law was British. On which insular thought she cut herself a large slice of fruit cake and sat back to enjoy it.

CHAPTER FIVE

It was easy for Sharley to settle down in the peaceful, secluded life of the *quinta*. Yet political revolutionaries outside this little world were threatening its existence, and Marcos had been forced to fight for the very heritage founded by his forefathers.

Though she could appreciate Marcos' point of view, she knew that if she listened to Pedro Lopez and his followers, she would be able to sympathise with them as well. It was her ability to see both sides of a story which made her such a good journalist, though it also meant she had no strong, independent views of her own.

'Maybe I don't have a viewpoint on anything,' she had once said to Sam Morris. 'Maybe I'm Miss Sweden—a perpetual neutral.'

Her editor had looked at her humorously. 'You'll be able to reach your own conclusion when it's necessary,' he had said. 'But until that day comes, just get the facts as they are and set them down.'

Thinking over Sam Morris's words, Sharley wondered whether one could ever be totally immune to outside influence. We are all the product of our own environment and traditions, she thought, and current trends must make some impression too. Not that they had made all that much headway in Portugal. Here was a country steeped in its own tradition; not only through its history, but through its religion as well, which still played such an important part in the lives of its people.   Sharley rarely gave any thought to religion. As a child she had received and accepted the instruction taught to her at school. But when she went to live in London, she found herself among people who had started to question the old beliefs and, as a result, she found herself doing the same. Although there was much which she still considered valid, there was a great deal she no longer believed, and she was in a state of flux.

Not so Marcos Santana. His rigid, old-fashioned background was no breeding place for doubts of any kind. That was why he was so self-opinionated and confident: believing that God could only be on his side.

On Sharley's first Sunday at the *quinta*, she came down for breakfast dressed in jeans and sweater. As she crossed the large hall, Marcos appeared from a room on her left. He wore a navy suit and pristine white shirt, and looked ready for a board meeting rather than for a day in the country.

'I am going to church,' he explained at her enquiring look, and stared disapprovingly at her jeans. 'I assumed you would accompany me.'

'I didn't know you went regularly.'

'I go every week. I will wait for you to change.'

She nibbled at her lip. 'I'm not sure I want to go.'

'Why not? Don't you believe in God?'

'I don't believe one has to go to church in order to pray.'

'I agree with you on that point,' he said, 'but I find one absorbs the atmosphere of prayer more easily in a church.'

Sharley was surprised, both by his explanation and the fact that he had deigned to give her one. But it seemed he still had more to say on the subject, for he spoke again.

'When we pray, we create a bond between ourselves and some unknown force, and it becomes even stronger when a group of people pray together. It's the way an electric current works. A single wire will only light a small lamp, but if you combine many wires, sufficient current can be generated to give power to a hundred lamps.'

'And you think that also applies to prayer?'

'I am sure of it. The greater the current we generate, the greater the power given to goodness.'

'Do you always believe you're on the side of goodness?'

'If you are asking me whether I believe everything I do to be right, then my answer is "Yes". Otherwise I would not be doing it, would I?' His teeth glimmered briefly in his dark skin, but it was more a sarcastic acknowledgment of her comment than a smile.

'Everyone always believes they're right,' Sharley retorted. 'In a war, both sides will often say they're fighting on God's side. Are you saying you believe that the side which wins is the one which God supports?'

'Unfortunately not. Very often might is stronger than right.'

'And evil flourishes over good,' she concluded.

'Sometimes,' Marcos replied quietly. 'I would like to continue this discussion, Charlotte, but it's getting late, and if you do not wish to come to church, I will go without you.'

A step on the stair made Sharley turn, and she saw Senhora Santana coming towards them, formally dressed in black, and wearing hat and gloves. She politely made no comment on Sharley's appearance and gave her a warm smile before turning to her son.

'I'm ready to leave when you are, Marcos.'

Inclining his head in Sharley's direction, Marcos languidly moved to the front door. His formal clothes emphasised his graceful walk, beneath which Sharley sensed the strength of steel.

A few moments later she was alone, and she went out to the verandah for breakfast. The weather was like high summer in England, but she knew that for Portugal it was seasonal, and that within a month she would be finding the heat uncomfortable—if, of course, she was still here. Somehow she thought she would be. If Marcos wanted her to stay, he would get his own way. If he could not use his authority to achieve what he wanted, he was not above using his charm.

Sharley poured out a cup of coffee and helped herself to a piece of fruit from one of the bowls. She could not help noting the perfection of the table appointments. The china was bone-thin and delicately patterned with flowers, and many of the serving dishes were silver: Georgian and impressive, and probably brought over from England by Marcos' Scottish mother.

Sharley mused on the strangeness of finding such a woman in these surroundings, and wondered what had brought Mrs Santana to Portugal originally. Had she met Marcos' father in Scotland? She tried to picture the man, but could only envisage an older version of the son. Marcos' mother had told her that portraits of the Santana ancestors were kept in the family residence in Lisbon, which Marcos was considering selling in favour of a small apartment.

'He's not particularly fond of Lisbon society,' Senhora Santana had explained, 'and only goes to the capital when business makes it necessary.'

'I can't see him as a countryman, though,' Sharley had said.

'Because you're judging him by his looks—which is what most women do,' Senhora Santana had replied. 'But his appearance does him an injustice.'

'In what way?'

'He has much more to him than a handsome face and body.'

The arrival of a servant had made it impossible for Senhora Santana to continue, and by the time the servant had left, the conversation had changed.

Sharley thought of their conversation as she finished her breakfast, and was uneasily aware that she was thinking too much of her stranger husband. Pushing back her chair, she debated whether to take a stroll or do some painting in the garden.

Deciding on the latter, she fetched her sketching pad and paints from her room, collected a jar of water, and went outside. Watercolour painting was her favourite hobby, and one she normally had little time to indulge in. But here she would not feel any guilt at spending long hours sketching and painting. After all, what else did she have to do? The thought of being a lady of leisure was intriguing, though she knew it would bore her if it went on too long.

Wandering slowly across the grass, she was reminded of the greenness of England, though she doubted whether this lawn would retain its lovely colour once the weather became hotter. Wherever she turned her eyes she was confronted with beauty, and she found it difficult to decide which scene to paint first. It was the heat which eventually made the decision for her, and with relief she settled on a bench in the shade beneath a gnarled old tree.

It was a beautiful day, the stillness interrupted only by the droning of insects. A pink-flowering rhododendron obscured the view to the left of her, but to the right the lawns fell away to reveal endless rows of carefully tended vines, which wound their way over undulating crests of land, some sufficiently steep to be described as hills. Narrow, well-kept roads made access to them easy, and she determined to do some exploring before the week was out.

Sharley was busy sketching when she heard a sound behind her. It was too early for Marcos to be returning from church, and as she turned round she saw a pretty girl approaching her, elegantly yet demurely dressed in black.

It was a colour beloved of women on the Iberian Pensinula, and she wondered if they wore it because they knew it enhanced their olive skins and lustrous eyes, or because they were perpetually in mourning for some relative or other. Mourning or not, black did well for this particular girl.

Deep brown eyes and raven hair threw into relief a skin so flawless that it looked like porcelain. Her features were equally fine, the nose small and straight, the mouth curved and full, and the natural length of her eyelashes needed no enhancement. Despite the careful understatement of her dress, it did not disguise well-shaped legs and a curvaceous figure, and Sharley wished she were not wearing jeans.

'Good morning,' she said clearly, wanting to prevent the girl from speaking Portuguese.

'Good morning,' the reply came back in precise English. 'I am Teresa Mateus.'

Sharley smiled, but was not sure if she should introduce herself as Marcos' wife. There was silence, and the Portuguese girl finally broke it.

'My father owns the neighbouring estate. You perhaps have seen it?'

'I drove past it the other day with Mrs Santana,' Sharley said, remembering a large, impressive-looking mansion. She recalled that her mother-in-law had lapsed into an unusual silence and now had a glimmering as to the reason. 'At the time it looked deserted,' she added.

'Only the servants were there. My parents and I have been in America for six weeks. But we returned home yesterday.' The girl looked around her. 'Is Marcos not here?'

'He hasn't returned from church.'

The girl perched herself carefully on the bench. 'You are a relation of Senhora Santana?'

Sharley hesitated, then said: 'I am her daughter-in-law.'

The dark eyes went blank, as if the girl did not understand. 'You are making a joke?' she asked quietly.

'It wasn't meant as a joke. I am Marcos' wife.' Sharley had not used these words before and they sounded strange to her.

To Teresa Mateus they seemed to be sabre thrusts. She blanched, and then rose slowly to her feet, not taking her eyes from Sharley's face.

'Why are you saying such a thing?' she choked. 'You cannot be Marcos' wife. It is impossible!'

'It's true. I'm sorry if it's come as a shock to you, but Marcos and I were married in London a week ago.'

Sharley rose too, and the girl backed away from her. The bloom had gone from her face and she looked pinched and older than her years. The news of Marcos' marriage had obviously upset her badly, and Sharley wondered if she were his girl-friend. Yet the thought of the autocratic Portuguese having one seemed so unlikely that she decided Teresa was far more likely to be his intended wife. If that were so, it would explain the silence that had befallen Mrs Santana as they had driven past the Mateus mansion a few days ago.

'We were married very suddenly,' Sharley explained gently. She was tempted to give the reasons for it, but knew that such a disclosure must come from Marcos. Whatever she herself said could only be misconstrued.

'I—I still cannot believe it.' The girl was still staring at her incredulously.

Sharley remained silent, though her thoughts were racing furiously. It was quite obvious that Marcos meant a great deal to Teresa Mateus, though it was equally obvious that the girl meant little to him. Had she done, he would surely have telephoned her in the States to tell

her of his unhappy predicament, and to warn her of what
he had to do.

With a deep sense of relief Sharley saw Marcos' tall,
slim figure in the distance, and she waved to him. He
quickened his pace, but slowed perceptibly as he turned a
bend in the path and saw Teresa. His exclamation of surprise was clearly audible, and he hurried the last few yards
towards them, then reached out to clasp the girl in greeting. He spoke Portuguese, and though Sharley could not
understand what he said, she determined to leave the
couple alone.

Gathering her painting things together, she went
silently across the lawn. Neither the man nor the girl took
notice of her, too intent on each other to be aware of her
departure. It was a fact which Sharley did not like, even
though she guessed that their absorption came from the
explanation Marcos was no doubt giving for his unexpected marriage.

For the next half hour Sharley remained in her bedroom. She changed into a dress and took unusual care
with her make-up, telling herself she was doing so as a
sign of respect for Senhora Santana, though she knew she
was doing it for Teresa Mateus. She might be a Santana
bride on sufferance, but there was no reason why she
should not be an attractive one. And she was definitely
that, she mused, eyeing herself in the mirror. Her week in
the sun had considerably lightened her hair, turning the
beige to streaky blonde, and she had also acquired a light
tan, which brought out the gold of her topaz eyes.

There was a knock on the door and Maria, the youngest
of the maids, entered. Her mother also worked at the
quinta, where Maria had been born and brought up. She
had played in the garden as a child and spent much of
her time with Mrs Santana, from whom she had learned
to speak English with a faint Scottish accent.

'Lunch is being served, *senhora*.'

'Good. I'm starving.' Sharley moved to the door, then became aware of Maria studying her. 'Is there anything wrong with the way I look?'

'Oh no, you are beautiful.' Shyly Maria touched the skirt of the soft apple-green silk dress Sharley was wearing. 'It is from your trousseau, yes?'

'I'm afraid not,' Sharley smiled. 'I bought it last year.'

She had treated herself to it when she had received a bonus for the front page coverage of one of her stories, and she was unexpectedly glad she had brought it with her. It was not only dark-haired *senhoritas* who could look feminine and appealing. Tucking her handkerchief into her bag, she ran quickly down the stairs.

Archways led into the main rooms—only Marcos' study having a door—and Sharley heard voices in the *sala* as she moved towards it. Marcos and his mother were standing with Teresa by the open windows, forming a triangle of intimacy which she was loath to disturb.

She paused on the threshold, not sure if she should back away and return later. She was still hesitating, when Senhora Santana turned her head and saw her.

'My dear, how pretty you look. Do come and join us.'

Sharley did so, giving the older woman a slight smile before glancing at Marcos, who seemed not to notice her appearance.

'You have already met Teresa, of course,' he said tonelessly.

'Of course,' Sharley replied, half mockingly, and saw him frown as he turned away from them and moved over to the drinks cabinet, an elaborately carved affair in oak.

Sharley followed him, knowing she had to speak to him alone.

'The news of our marriage was a tremendous shock to Senhorita Mateus,' she said softly. 'I think you should have warned her about it.'

'I did not expect her back so soon.' Marcos kept his voice low as he deftly poured golden liquid into a tall glass and handed it to her.

Sharley looked enquiringly at it.

'It's something new which I am perfecting,' he explained.

'A cocktail?'

'No,' he said disapprovingly. 'I detest such things. It usually means an unhappy mixture of different spirits.'

'Like a bad marriage.' She raised the glass to her lips. 'It's delicious,' she said.

'Like a good marriage,' he replied.

His dry humour caught her by surprise and she almost choked on her drink.

'You have not seen me under the best circumstances, Charlotte,' he went on. 'I am not always so determined and serious.'

'You could have fooled me,' she quipped. 'Even the first time we met, I found you extremely rude.'

'I had—still have—many problems.'

'Won't the merger with Uncle George help you?'

'Certainly. But the problems won't vanish overnight.'

'You have one big problem right in your own back yard,' she pointed out.

'I beg your pardon?'

Seeing he did not understand the metaphor, she allowed her eyes to move to the girl talking to his mother. His gaze followed hers, and once again he looked secretive and withdrawn.

'Have you told Senhorita Mateus the truth?' Sharley asked.

'No.'

'Why not?'

'Because I do not wish to disclose the sordid details of the affair,' he said curtly. 'She would be hurt.'

Sharley's cheeks flamed at the recollection of the embarrassing photographs.

'Not more so than she is now,' she retorted. 'I'm sure she'd feel much happier if she knew you didn't marry me out of love.'

'It is no concern of Teresa how I feel towards my wife.'

'Don't be stupid,' Sharley said crossly. 'All you have to do is tell her we were drugged. Then she won't think you took me to bed because you fancied me.'

His sharply indrawn breath told her he was furious at her frankness. In his world, such sexual discussions were no doubt frowned upon.

'I suppose I've shocked you,' she said, facing him bravely.

'Only because your temper is unnecessary. I am not unaware of what happens between a man and woman, Charlotte, though I do not think one need express it as bluntly as you do. But why we were in bed, and why we married, must remain a secret between ourselves and my mother.'

'And the man who precipitated the whole thing,' Sharley reminded him.

'That is so,' Marcos agreed, his lips thinning with distaste. 'But no one else must know. No one. I have already told you why we must maintain the pretence at all times, and that also applies to "all friends".'

'But Teresa will be so hurt.'

'That is *my* problem, not yours. So please, from now on, try to act the loving bride.'

'I'm not a good enough actress for that.'

His eyes glittered. 'Do you wish me to give you some lessons?'

Sharley's temper rose higher. 'What a heartless brute you are! If you had any feelings for Teresa you would tell her the truth.'

'And have the whole of Portuguese society know of it in twenty-four hours?'

'I'm sure she'd keep it a secret if you asked her.'

'Women cannot keep secrets.'

'*I* can.'

His look was so easy for her to read that her face flamed. 'I may not be *your* idea of a woman, Marcos Santana, but thank heavens your opinion of me doesn't matter.'

'That applies the other way too,' he said icily. 'But you must still obey my orders. Now let us join the others. And please do not make a scene. Remember, you are supposed to be a lady.'

Sharley glared at him as he placed his hand on her arm and led her across the room. The urge to pull away from him was strong, but she resisted it, knowing he would only be amused. Why did she dislike him so much? After all, he had treated her with respect. It must be his arrogant inflexibility, she concluded.

'I see Marcos has given you his new drink to taste,' Senhora Santana commented as her son and Sharley approached them. 'You should feel honoured. He doesn't let many people try it. He wants to wait until it's completely ready to be marketed.'

'Is it wrong to wish for perfection, Mae?' he asked.

'You know it isn't. As long as you realise that perfection is rarely found.'

'Champagne is perfection for me,' Teresa came prettily into the conversation.

Sharley looked at her. In the hour since they had first met in the garden, the girl had regained her composure, which meant that either Senhora Santana had given her a hint of the true state of affairs between her son and his bride, or else the girl was adept at hiding her feelings. Remembering Marcos' assertion that no one should know the real position between himself and his bride, she could only assume that the stage had lost a great actress in Teresa.

'Do *you* like champagne, my dear?' Senhora Santana's voice broke into Sharley's thoughts.

'Charlotte prefers something more astringent,' Marcos replied before she could answer. 'It can also be seen in the colours she wears: the sharpness of green, the acidity of lemon.'

'And black,' Sharley added sweetly, 'or would you be happier to see me in scarlet?'

'Scarlet?' Teresa echoed. 'Doesn't that have a special significance?'

'To be a scarlet woman is to be considered a female of loose morals,' Marcos said pedantically. 'But Charlotte is teasing us. You know how strange the English sense of humour can be.'

'*I'm* English,' his mother reminded him.

'You are Scottish,' he corrected.

Maria's entry to say luncheon was ready put an end to the conversation, and with relief Sharley moved into the dining room.

For the first half of the meal Marcos gave most of his attention to Teresa, enquiring about her trip to the States and listening to her chatter with as much interest as if she were discoursing on port wine. But halfway through the main course he fixed his piercing dark eyes upon Sharley's plate.

'You have not touched your food. Is it not to your liking?'

'I'm not hungry. It must be the hot weather,' she replied, reluctant to explain she always lost her appetite when she was under stress. Yet why should she be upset because of her argument with Marcos? Perhaps her phoney marriage was more of a strain on her than she realised. Without question Marcos' proximity always unnerved her. He seemed to make her tense and angry, and there was absolutely no rapport between them.

It was a relief when Teresa spoke. 'Many English-women are very thin,' she announced, as if she had made a discovery.

'There is a vast difference between being thin and slim,' Sharley replied. 'Anglo-Saxons find Latin races too plump.'

'The ideal woman for a happy man is—his wife,' Marcos replied.

Teresa's hand shook on her fork and Sharley was stirred to pity. Why did Marcos have to be so cruel? And why couldn't Teresa hide her affection for him? He really was a swine. She was sorry for any woman who loved him.

'I will have to leave you for a while this afternoon,' Marcos said abruptly. 'I have a business appointment in Oporto.'

'On a Sunday?' his mother asked in surprise.

'I have to meet some American importers, and Sunday is like any other day of the week to them.'

'How uncivilised they are!' Teresa frowned.

'They are sufficiently civilised to enjoy drinking Santana port wine,' Marcos commented.

'Then I will drink a toast to them,' Teresa said diplomatically, and raised her glass.

'I will take you home on my way,' Marcos told her.

'Thank you, but it won't be necessary. Mae and Pai are calling for me.'

'Please tell them I am sorry I was not here to greet them.'

'You must come to visit us. They are looking forward to seeing you.'

'Of course,' he said carefully, not looking directly at Teresa. 'I am looking forward to introducing my bride to them. Which reminds me, Mae, we must have a party to introduce Charlotte to all our friends.'

'It will be better if we have a reception in Lisbon,' his mother said. 'Our house there is far more suitable.'

'I wasn't thinking of a reception, Marcos' soft voice had an edge to it. 'I wish for something less formal.'

'Why? What's wrong with giving a big party? You've worked hard for your money and you shouldn't be ashamed of having it.'

'I would rather we did not continue this discussion,' Marcos said.

'You always say that when you feel you're losing an argument, *darling*,' Sharley said sweetly.

'I am glad you are intelligent enough to recognise it, my *love*,' he responded. 'It means you will know when not to argue with me.'

Promptly at two-thirty he left for his appointment, and Sharley remained a little longer in the *sala*, drinking coffee and listening to Teresa prattling on about her visit to New Orleans. Sharley had the impression that the girl thoroughly disapproved of the American way of life. She was full of criticism of the casual way the women dressed, the way they brought up their children, and she particularly disapproved of the large choice of tinned and frozen foods in the supermarkets.

'I do not understand why so many American women go out to work,' Teresa said firmly, turning to Sharley. 'They should be content to stay at home and look after their husbands and children.'

'Most of them do, until their children go to school,' Sharley informed her. 'But after that, why shouldn't they work, if that's what they want? Most women these days are as educated as their husbands, and if they want to utilise their ability outside the home, why shouldn't they? They may also need the money.'

'I still do not think that career women are attractive,'

Teresa remarked, refusing to be swayed by logic.

Sharley laughed outright. 'What about film and stage actresses? They're career women, aren't they?'

'A Portuguese man would not wish to marry such a woman. I am talking of the men in my circle,' Teresa added.

Sharley wanted to say that few American or British women—from any circle—would choose a Portuguese husband, but she discreetly kept quiet. The last thing she wanted was to quarrel with this silly, vacuous young woman.

Feigning a yawn of tiredness, she asked her mother-in-law's permission to retire to her room, and went upstairs.

The approaching afternoon threatened to be long and boring, and she wished she had brought her typewriter with her, so that she could do some writing. It had been years since she had had a long holiday, and the prospect of it going on for six months appalled her.

If her marriage to Marcos had been genuine, the situation would be quite different. She would have had many things to occupy her time; taking care of the man she loved, cooking special dishes for him, having his children, learning about his business interests. She tried to picture Marcos with children. She envisaged slim, hazel-eyed boys with haughty expressions, which would disappear when they became boisterous and gay. Somehow these thoughts were disquieting, and she dismissed them from her mind.

Sharley walked across to her bedside table and picked up a magazine. She had brought it with her from London because it contained a review on the political and business life in Portugal which she felt might be informative.

Sighing, she settled down in her chair for a quiet read. It seemed as if this was going to be her main activity for the rest of her stay in this country.

CHAPTER SIX

At four o'clock Sharley went down to the *sala* for tea. As she crossed the hall a maid appeared from the kitchen, wheeling a large teak tea-trolley laid with the silver tea-set, as well as a silver coffee service, and the usual liberal assortment of sandwiches and cakes. Sharley slowed down to let the girl precede her, realising nervously that other visitors must have arrived during her absence.

As she entered the *sala*, Dona Ana greeted her with a smile. 'Sharley, my dear, I'd like you to meet some very dear friends of mine, Senhor and Senhora Mateus, Teresa's parents.'

Sharley went forward to greet them. Senhora Mateus was a self-satisfied looking woman, the delicacy of her bones blurred by plumpness. But she had the same lustrous eyes as her daughter, and her hair was dark and glossy without a hint of grey. Senhor Mateus was also plump and black haired, and he and his wife reminded Sharley of a couple of well-fed pigeons. Senhora Mateus spoke little English, though her husband was more fluent, albeit pedantic, and he asked Sharley whether she had visited Portugal previously and how she enjoyed living here.

Sharley answered him politely, sensing from the way he looked at her that he was wondering what had attracted Marcos—whom he had in all probability regarded as his future son-in-law—to marry her.

As she rose to help serve the tea, she was also aware of the latent hostility which emanated from Teresa and her mother, and though it made her feel uncomfortable, she could not blame them for it. Marcos should have had enough trust in Teresa to explain the circumstances behind his marriage. If he cared for the girl, surely he would want her to know that in a few months his marriage would be annulled and he would be completely free?

Accepting her own cup of tea from Dona Ana, Sharley sat down again. Teresa did not look her way and was having a lively conversation in Portuguese with her hostess, leaving Sharley to wonder exactly how the girl regarded Marcos' marriage. Does she believe he found me so desirable that I was able to seduce him into it? she thought. Surely Teresa knows he prefers women of his own nationality? She tried to imagine Marcos being so swayed by passion that his normal attitudes deserted him, and found the idea disturbing. It was much easier for her to see him as icy cool and uncaring.

'Marcos told me you are a goddaughter of Sir George Fawcett,' Teresa said softly, unexpectedly turning to Sharley.

Sharley nodded, wondering whether Marcos had told Teresa this in order to give his wife a little social importance.

'He's my mother's cousin,' she explained.

'You are lucky to have such an important person as your relative.'

'I'm lucky to have someone as *nice* as my relative as godfather,' Sharley replied.

'Was it through Sir George that you met Marcos?' Teresa's hostile eyes were still fixed on her.

'In a way.'

Teresa slid across the settee, making it easier for her to speak in a low voice. 'You are fortunate that Marcos needed to push forward his merger with a British company. Otherwise he would never have married you.'

'Is that what he told you?' Sharley asked blandly, not sure if Marcos had indeed confided in Teresa.

'Not quite in those words,' the girl admitted, 'but I was

able to read between the lines. I assure you that you have no chance of happiness with Marcos. He is not a man who likes to feel he has been coerced into any situation. You may be his wife, but he does not love you, and you will never be able to make him happy.'

The gratuitous rudeness of the remarks made Sharley lose her temper. 'He obviously didn't think *you* could either,' she retorted, and was delighted to see a flush stain the olive-skinned cheeks.

'Marcos didn't marry me because he still thought I was too young. He wanted me to see more of life. In Portugal, a marriage is considered binding until death, which is not the case in your country.' Teresa's eyes glittered triumphantly as she continued: 'Marcos told me he did not marry you in a church.'

'Because there was no time.'

Sharley did not know why she bothered to continue the conversation. A moment ago she had felt sufficient compassion for Teresa to want her to know the truth. Yet here she was perpetuating the myth that love had been the reason for Marcos' precipitate marriage. Maybe it was because she found Teresa's bluntness astonishingly rude.

'There was no time to call the banns,' she continued, 'and as Marcos wanted to marry me immediately, a register office was the only solution.'

Teresa was not to be deterred. 'I do not believe Marcos would have had any other kind of ceremony with you.'

With an effort Sharley resisted the urge to pour her cup of tea over Teresa's impeccably coiffed head. Even if the girl knew that Marcos' marriage was an expedient one, she had no right to talk so rudely to the girl who had helped him. And if she did not know the true reason for it, then her behaviour was even more disgraceful.

'If you have any further comments to make on my

marriage,' Sharley said acidly, 'I suggest you make them to Marcos.'

'You must invite Senhora Santana to our home,' Senhor Mateus called across to his daughter.

'I was just doing that, Pai,' Teresa lied with a promptness that astonished Sharley.

'I don't expect to do much visiting for the next few months,' Sharley said to Senhor Mateus, taking the opportunity of moving to one of the other chairs. 'I would like to learn as much as possible about my husband's estate.'

'You are acquainted with the port wine business, *senhora*?'

'Unfortunately not. But I wish to learn.'

'With Marcos to teach you, you will soon become an expert,' said Dona Ana, coming into the conversation.

'I don't think I'll ever be an expert.'

'Don't be so sure,' Senhor Mateus smiled. 'Port wine is the most important commodity in your husband's life, and you should not underestimate its potency.'

Sharley laughed. 'On the vine or on the table?'

'In both places.'

'I think we should go home, Pai,' said Teresa, interrupting Sharley and her father disapprovingly.

Sharley gave the girl a beaming smile before turning back to the man. 'As soon as I've settled down here, *senhor*, I shall be delighted to accept your kind invitation.'

'Good,' he said, oblivious of his daughter's annoyance, and in a flurry of handshaking the Mateus family departed.

'It was good to see Senhor Mateus after so long an absence,' Dona Ana commented when she returned from seeing her visitors off. 'He's an intelligent man and he and Maria were very kind to me when my husband died.'

'Senhora Mateus and Teresa bear a striking resemblance to one another,' Sharley replied. 'Are they alike in character?'

'Not in the least. Maria is an uncomplicated, gentle person, but Teresa is very shrewd and thrives on admiration.' The grey-green eyes, so much like Marcos', twinkled. 'I can see you don't like her.'

'I don't. I think she could cause trouble.'

Dona Ana looked surprised. 'I can't say I've ever thought of Teresa in that light.'

'Perhaps I'm not being fair to her,' Sharley said quickly. 'She's obviously been badly shocked by Marcos' marriage.'

Dona Ana sighed. 'She's been in love with him since she was a schoolgirl.'

'And how does your son feel about her?' Sharley asked, taking the bull by the horns. She saw Dona Ana hesitate. 'Please don't try to be diplomatic with me, *senhora*. I think it's important for us not to have any pretence about my marriage. We did it for a specific reason and we'll annul it as soon as we can.'

'I suppose you're right to be so prosaic about it,' Dona Ana sighed. 'But I still think of you as Marcos' wife, and who knows, you may decide—you may both decide that——'

'No,' Sharley cut in flatly. 'Neither of us would want it to be permanent. That's why I was so surprised when Marcos said he didn't want to tell Teresa the truth.'

'Because he thinks women can't keep a secret. He's told you that himself.'

'I know. But if Teresa is as shrewd as you say, I think she *could* be discreet.'

'I doubt if you can convince Marcos.'

'No one can convince him of anything. He's too obstinate.'

'Only with you,' his mother smiled. 'But that's because he's on the defensive. You worry him.' The woman hesitated before continuing. 'He's very aware of you, my dear, and I'm delighted by it. If you and he were to . . . Oh, I'm sure you know what I mean.'

'I do,' Sharley admitted, grinning. 'You said the same thing about ten seconds ago. But it's a pipe dream, Dona Ana.'

'Are you sure? I like you so much, my dear. I wish with all my heart that your marriage to my son could be a lasting one.'

Sharley was moved by the words, though she could not help wondering whether Dona Ana might have said them to any another English girl.

'It isn't only because you're a fellow countrywoman of mine,' the older woman continued, as if she knew what was passing through Sharley's mind. 'I'm sure many English girls would love to be Marcos' wife, but I feel instinctively that you're the right one for him.'

'I'm afraid your instinct is wrong this time,' Sharley replied. 'Marcos and I rub each other the wrong way.'

'I can't answer for my son,' Dona Ana shrugged, 'but I often feel you deliberately say things to annoy him.'

'I don't have to say very much. He dislikes everything I stand for. He said so.'

'Everything you stand for?'

'The fact that I work and that I'm a feminist,' Sharley explained.

Dona Ana looked surprised. 'He doesn't mean it—I'm sure of that. Why, he's always encouraged women to go out and do things for themselves.'

'Really?' Sharley exclaimed disbelievingly.

'He was responsible for persuading my late husband's brother to send his two daughters to university,' Dona Ana went on. 'And if you think my son old-fashioned, wait until you meet his uncle! He hasn't yet left the ark.'

Sharley chuckled. 'Marcos isn't *that* old-fashioned,'

she agreed, 'but——'

'There is no "but",' came the firm reply. 'He's a far more liberal thinker than you give him credit for.'

Sharley still found this difficult to concede. Obviously her mother-in-law had lived in Portugal so long that she was unaware of the modern man's attitude towards women. Perhaps Marcos was considered free-thinking in Portugal, but he would certainly not be thought so in any other part of the Western world.

'Teresa will make your son a much better wife than I ever could,' she said impulsively, for even though she did not like the girl, she felt it was important to speak the truth. 'Once Marcos has finalised the business merger with my uncle, there won't be any need for me to stay here.'

'Sometimes I think it might be better if Marcos left too,' Dona Ana said. 'When those evil people drugged you both, they might easily have murdered you. And if they'd murdered my son, the Santana company could immediately have been taken over by the rebels.'

The thought had also crossed Sharley's mind, particularly when she had realised Marcos had no brothers to follow in his footsteps.

'Are there any other members of the family in the business?' she asked.

'Only Marcos' uncle, whom I've just mentioned. But he has no son, and my husband and I only had one child.' The woman walked around the room, her dark silk dress moving gracefully round her. 'It's a pity for a woman to have only one child. She worries all the time about his health and his happiness.' She stopped and looked across at Sharley. 'I'd feel so much happier if he left Portugal and settled in Scotland.'

'I can't ever see him doing that,' Sharley stated. 'This land is his home. He loves every inch of it.'

'He could still be happy in Scotland,' his mother persisted. 'When my father dies, he'll inherit a large estate—far bigger than the one he has here.'

'Bigger?'

'Yes, my dear. I am an only child too, and everything my father has will be left to Marcos. He will inherit a title and estates of which he can be proud.'

'He has a great deal to be proud of here too.' Sharley looked through the window at the rolling landscape. 'I can understand why he doesn't want to leave.'

'One day he'll have to make a decision between staying on here or returning to claim his heritage in Scotland. That's why I was pleased when he decided to merge the Santana Company with a British one. It would make it so much easier for him to live in Scotland.'

'Do you think that prompted the merger?'

'No. He did it in order to consolidate his position here. But the day will come when someone *will* have to make a deal with Lopez or with his successor. The workers in this country have been suppressed for too long, and now that their chance for freedom has come, they won't relinquish it.'

'I don't blame them,' Sharley said, and then looked rueful. 'Marcos would be furious if he heard me say such a thing!'

'No, he wouldn't. I've already told you, he feels the same way.'

'I find that hard to believe,' Sharley replied frankly. 'Your son seems such an awful snob.'

'My dear, you know him so little,' Dona Ana expostulated. 'I wish you could see him without prejudice. If you could, you would realise how much you're misjudging him.'

Later, as Sharley strolled along one of the narrow paths between the vines, she pondered on Dona Ana's view of Marcos, and doubted if it could ever be her own. The more she knew of her stranger husband, the more alien and dislikeable he appeared. And another fact had emerged today: he had no perception where women were concerned—especially Teresa. How could he see her as innocent and old-fashioned?

Sharley bent to touch a large cluster of grapes. They were heavy, and a deep purple bloom lay upon their skin. She picked one and put it into her mouth, then pulled a face, for it was sharp and full of pips.

'They'll taste much sweeter when they are fully ripened,' a soft voice said, and she looked round and saw Marcos watching her in the deepening dusk. He seemed taller and his face was thinner too, though this could have been due to the pallor of fatigue.

'You look as if the discussions didn't go too well,' she said impulsively, then regretted having spoken as she saw him frown.

'They were unpleasant,' he replied. 'Though they gave me a great deal of satisfaction.' He paused, then said clearly: 'I saw Pedro Lopez this afternoon, and returned the photographs to him.'

Sharley swallowed hard. 'I—I thought you were seeing some Americans?'

'I did not wish to worry you or my mother with the truth. But now that the meeting is over, I decided to tell you.'

'What happened?'

Marcos' broad shoulders lifted. 'Lopez looked extremely embarrassed and said how much he regretted that the pictures had been taken.'

'What a liar,' she exclaimed angrily.

'That's what I thought.'

'I wish I'd known you were going to see him. I'd have liked to come with you.'

The flicker of a smile lifted the corners of Marcos'

...th, and Sharley could not help noticing how well shaped it was. Quickly she directed her thoughts elsewhere.

'I hope he realises he won't be able to blackmail you in the future,' she said.

'I hope so too. But with a man like Lopez, one can never tell. He is not the type to give up easily.'

Sharley continued to walk along the path through the vineyard, and Marcos fell into step beside her.

'He still wishes the workers to participate in our company's profits,' he went on, 'and he has warned me there may be more trouble if I refuse to meet his terms. But fortunately the majority of the men in my employ are loyal and, as long as I'm here, I will have their support. It's my children who may not find it,' he added.

Sharley glanced at him, but he did not look her way.

'My children,' he repeated. 'My sons.'

'You'll need a wife first.'

'Is that an offer?'

'Do you think it likely?' she asked icily.

One of his dark eyebrows lifted. 'I am considered highly eligible.'

She gave an exclamation. 'How conceited you are!'

'Because I know that women are attracted to me?'

'What women?'

'All kinds.' He eyed her with unusual amusement. 'Even English ones.'

'Then how have you remained a bachelor so long?' Sharley demanded.

'Perhaps I haven't found what I'm looking for in a woman.'

She thought of Teresa and her explanation of why Marcos had not yet married her. 'I still think you should have told Teresa the truth about us,' she said. 'It's unkind to let her believe you married me because my godfather is

Sir George Fawcett.'

'Is that what she told you?' He stopped and looked at her in surprise.

'She delighted in telling me so,' Sharley emphasised. 'And also in warning me that my marriage won't last.'

'Then you should feel reassured.'

'I don't need reassurance from Teresa.'

'Are you certain you didn't misunderstand her?'

'Quite sure.'

They walked a further ten yards in silence.

'I had no desire to tell Teresa the whole truth,' Marcos said suddenly. 'But I felt I had to give her some explanation as to why I had married you so suddenly.'

Sharley pulled a face. 'Teresa is counting the days until you're free of me.'

'You make it sound as if she actually said so.'

'She did. And much more besides.'

'I find that hard to believe,' he said quietly. 'Teresa is a simple girl, pretty and uncomplicated.'

'Uncomplicated as a fox! If you intend to marry her, you'd do well to know it.'

'I don't see her in the same way you do.'

'Then you're blind. Once she's married you, she'll lead you by the nose.'

'Do you think so?' he asked coolly. 'I have yet to meet the woman capable of doing that.'

Sharley tossed her head. 'I'd love to be around the day she pulls the rope and cracks the whip.'

'When that time comes, you won't be here.'

They came to the end of the path, which then divided in two directions. Marcos took the left fork and Sharley, not anticipating him, turned right. She had taken several paces before she realised he was not beside her. She stopped and glanced over her shoulder. Marcos too had stopped and was looking at her with the faintest of smiles.

'Trust you,' he murmured, and in a few quick strides came abreast of her. 'Are you always so contrary?'

'Not always,' she said, treating the remark with apparent seriousness, and not wanting to give him the satisfaction of knowing she was aware of his teasing. 'But generally so with men.'

'Is it because you aren't prepared to give them what they ask for?' he questioned.

'What do you mean?'

Marcos lowered his lids. 'Forget it. I had no right to ask you that. Please forgive me.'

'I'm not offended.' Sharley kept her voice casual. 'But don't make the mistake of thinking that because I believe in women's equality, I also believe they should have the same sexual freedom as men.'

'Don't you?' He stared at her intently. 'Why not?'

'Because men can have sex without love, and it doesn't affect them. But women can't. Promiscuity makes them hard and—oh, different somehow. I have other reasons too,' she added, 'but I don't think there's any point in discussing them.'

'You have answered my question,' he said. 'Thank you.' He went on looking at her. In the dusk his eyes were gleaming, though their colour was not discernible. 'I am glad you have certain inhibitions, Charlotte.'

'Why do you persist in calling me Charlotte?' she asked.

'Why not? I don't think Sharley suits you.'

He reached out and pulled her against his side. Startled by the unexpectedness of his action, Sharley was too surprised to move. It was only as she felt the hardness of his body along the whole length of her thigh that she tried to edge away from him. But his grip tightened on her.

'Please let me go, Marcos.'

'Is it wrong for a man to hold his wife?'

'I'm only your wife in name.'

'It's an important name,' he replied. 'Most women would be proud to bear it.' As he spoke he loosened his grip, but only in order to turn her round to face him. 'How defensive you are with me,' he murmured. 'What are you afraid of?'

'Nothing.'

'Then you won't mind if I go on holding you?'

'I'll mind very much.' Sharley's anger was rising. 'I'm not a toy for you to play with, Marcos. Please let me go.'

Ignoring her request, he lowered his head until their lips met.

The instant she felt their pressure, Sharley knew Marcos was as proficient in lovemaking as he was in everything else. His touch was sure, his hands gentle yet firm as they moved down her back and came to rest upon her hips. Only then did their grip tighten as he pulled her body closer to his and let her feel his mounting need.

He was too strong for Sharley to fight him. She could make an attempt, but she was afraid it would only succeed in amusing him, and might even arouse him to greater passion. Because of this, she remained motionless in his hold, hoping her lack of response would show the contempt in which she held him.

But he did not appear to mind her passivity, and one of his hands came up to play with her hair, twining a long tress around his fingers, while he moved his mouth along the curve of her cheek and across the side of her throat.

'How thin you are,' he said. 'I feel as if I'm holding a bird in my hands.'

It was not a sentiment she could echo, for there was nothing birdlike about Marcos. He had an animal magnetism which she found overpowering. His indolence had vanished and she knew it to be a mask which he used to hide his strength. Even his drawling voice gave no hint of the passion which lurked behind the urbane façade.

But now the façade had vanished, and he was making no effort to disguise his desire for her. She felt his passion increasing and, instead of being pleased to know she could arouse him, she was furious at his lack of control. He would never behave this way with Teresa; she was certain of that. He would have held himself aloof in case he frightened her. Yet with herself, whom he had cajoled—no, practically forced—into marrying, he was deliberately showing his desire.

Fury lent strength to her arms and she pushed hard against his chest.

'Stop it, Marcos! I don't want you to kiss me. Let me go!'

She tried to twist away from his mouth, but though her lips managed to avoid his, the curve of her throat was open to him, and he grasped it between his thumb and forefinger and pressed lightly below her ears.

'Why do you fight me, Charlotte? I only want to kiss you.'

'I don't want your kisses.' She sought for a way of hurting him. 'I don't fancy you, Marcos. You leave me cold. Can't you understand that?'

For an instant she thought he was not going to listen to her, then his hands dropped to his sides and he stepped back. The dusk had given way to a deeper gloom and Sharley was sorry she could not see the expression on his face. Yet she was glad too, for it meant he could not see hers either.

'Forgive me, Charlotte. I am not in the habit of kissing an unwilling woman.'

'You could have fooled *me*. I thought I'd made my unwillingness perfectly clear the minute you grabbed me, but you took no notice.'

Turning on her heel, she walked towards the house,

and had only gone a few paces when Marcos caught up with her.

'Forgive me, Charlotte,' he said again, his voice low and embarrassed. 'I don't know what happened to me. Blame it on the mood of the afternoon, and the fact that I still find it strange to have a wife.'

'You should regard me as a business partner,' she flashed back. 'That's how I feel about *you*. An unwilling partner, I might add.'

He sighed heavily. 'I appreciate your feelings, and . . .' He touched her arm lightly with his fingers, drawing them back instantly as he felt her flinch. 'From the moment we met I felt you were a young woman of sensibility. Please take my word that from now on, I will treat you as such.'

Sharley did not find Marcos' assessment of her character as much of a compliment as he evidently meant it to be. 'A young woman of sensibility.' How prosaic and practical it made her seem! He would never apply such a description to Teresa.

Irritably aware that she would be unsatisfied no matter how he treated her—furious at any passion he might display, and equally so at his efforts to reassure her she would not be subjected to it again—she was far from behaving with any sensibility, and she almost ran the last few steps into the *quinta*.

Only when she was in the hall again did any semblance of calm return, and she looked up at him without giving away any of her inner turmoil.

'Let's forget this ever happened, Marcos. I came here to help you, and I won't go back on my word. But if you ever touch me again, I'll walk out. Is that clear?'

'As crystal,' he replied, and watched unsmilingly as she turned round and went steadily up the stairs to her room.

CHAPTER SEVEN

SHARLEY had thought she might be embarrassed when she saw Marcos again. But when she came down to the *sala* later that evening, he greeted her so casually she almost thought the incident in the vineyard had been a figment of her imagination.

He was having a drink with his mother, and her pulse quickened as he turned and saw her, then walked leisurely over to the cabinet to pour her a sherry. As he handed it to her their fingers met, and a tingle like an electric shock went through her arm. But she realised the sensation was only hers, for Marcos looked quite unconcerned as he gave her a brief smile and returned to sit beside his mother, continuing the conversation which Sharley's appearance had interrupted.

She sat down and listened to them with interest. They were talking about the estate, and she was surprised to hear how knowledgeable Dona Ana was about it. She was talking animatedly about an American wine shipper who had visited the *quinta* two months previously and had now sent them a large order.

'It isn't only the order that pleases me so much,' Dona Ana said happily, 'but also the fact that Mr Heron intends doing a great deal of publicity. If port wine could become as familiar to Americans as Coca-Cola——'

Marcos' laugh interrupted his mother's flow, and she looked at him indignantly.

'You're too casual, Marcos. You should show a little more enthusiasm.'

'I'm too old a hand at this game to be carried away by someone's promise.'

'It's far more than a promise. You've just been given the biggest order we've ever had from the States, and Mr Heron has now invited you over to visit him. He's promised to get you on to television, and if you used your title——'

'No,' Marcos cut in firmly. 'That is out of the question.'

'I didn't even know you had a title.' Sharley looked at him. 'Why don't you use it?'

'Because I consider titles outmoded—unless one has earned it for oneself.'

As Sharley had thought Marcos the sort of man to enjoy using a title, his comment surprised her. No sooner did she think she was beginning to know him than he did— or said—something which showed her how wrong she was.

'I'm sorry you find it difficult to change your image of me,' he murmured softly.

'What makes you say that?'

'Sometimes you are easy to read.'

'Tell me more,' she mocked lightly.

He rose, empty glass in hand. 'I know you think of me as a domineering autocrat who forced you into marriage and took you away to a foreign land.'

'Don't be silly, Marcos,' his mother said behind him. 'You had a perfectly good reason for acting the way you did. There's no need to make yourself sound like an abductor.'

'But in Charlotte's eyes that's exactly what I am. Isn't that so?' he asked, still looking at her.

'I came willingly,' Sharley replied.

'You came,' he agreed. 'But not "willingly".'

Sharley was not sure how to reply to this, and was luckily forestalled by the entry of a manservant to say dinner was served.

This was always the most elaborate meal of the day, though Dona Ana had told Sharley that in many Portuguese households the main meal was served at lunchtime.

'But Marcos is always so busy during the day,' she had explained, 'that he resents stopping for more than half an hour.'

Even this was an over-estimation, for in the two weeks since Sharley had lived here, he had only had lunch at the *quinta* on three occasions; preferring to take a picnic meal with him, which he would eat in the vineyards.

The estate was so vast that Sharley had only seen a small part of it. She was keen to explore it all, but knew she would need a car for this, and was reluctant to ask Marcos for the loan of one. Yet why should she be? She had no reason to be scared of him. After all, he was her husband.

Surreptitiously she watched him. How much the master he looked, sitting at the head of the long table. His surroundings suited him well; the rich, sombre decor of the room; the wall lamps that glowed behind his head, making his hair look blacker and shinier than ever; the light of the candles—which flamed in the silver candelabra down the centre of the table—accentuating the bronze of his face. All the furniture was on a grand scale, though the rooms were so large that this was not noticeable until one realised how out of place the individual pieces would be in the normal-sized house.

With a start Sharley realised Marcos had been speaking to her. 'I'm afraid I was miles away,' she apologised. 'What did you say?'

'That I have to go to Lisbon for a few days and won't be back until Friday.'

He paused, and Sharley wondered whether he was going to ask her to accompany him. But he picked up his fork and resumed eating.

'Do you go to Lisbon often?' she asked.

'Yes. I have many friends there.'

Sharley was curious to know if he was going for social reasons this time, but he did not proffer any further information, although the quick glance he gave her told her he was aware of her curiosity.

Resentfully she continued to eat. She was no more curious than any girl would have been in similar circumstances. Marcos obviously had a private life of his own with which he was not going to allow his enforced marriage to interfere. Yet though they both knew their marriage was a mockery, it would surely make it more difficult for him to pursue the interests he had led before.

She wished she knew more about Portuguese social life, and whether the men here had the same sexual freedom as men in the rest of Europe. Portugal was a predominantly religious society, where marriage was still considered to be sacred, and she doubted if girls of good family would indulge in affairs. Still, there were always women available, and she supposed Marcos would find his companionship from among them.

Sharley glanced at him out of the corner of her eye. He was talking to his mother and his face, in semi-profile, made him look older and more alert. He wore his hair slightly long, though it stopped short of his crisp white collar and lay smoothly behind his well-shaped ears.

Somehow she found it hard to believe that if Marcos loved Teresa he would want to wait until she was more mature before marrying her. He was the sort of man who would be only too happy to marry an innocent young girl and teach her about love and life. That he had not done so proved to her once again what an enigmatic character he was.

'I shall be quite happy to take you to Lisbon with me if

you wish to come along.' Marcos interrupted Sharley's thoughts again, and she regarded him with surprise.

'Wouldn't I be in the way?'

'On the contrary. You would relieve the tedium.'

Sharley did not like the idea of being used as an antidote to boredom; as a compliment, she had had better.

'I thought you were going on a social visit,' she said lightly.

'No. It's purely business. I didn't mention it because I didn't think you'd be interested.'

'I'm more likely to be interested in your business than in your private life.'

His eyes glittered, black as jet caught in the light, and Sharley realised she had been abrupt and rude.

'I only meant that I—that I don't think the social side of your life is my concern,' she explained.

'All of my life is your concern as long as you are my wife,' Marcos replied.

She looked away from him, at the same time aware of the expression on Dona Ana's face: a mixture of amusement and surprise which then gave way to perplexity.

'If Sharley goes with you to Lisbon,' the woman said to her son, 'you won't be able to stay with Fernandez.' She glanced at Sharley. 'My brother-in-law recently gave up his large house and has moved into a penthouse on the outskirts of the city. It's smaller than his previous home, and if you decided to stay there, you and Marcos would have to share a room.'

Sharley's face flamed with embarrassment, and Marcos also looked taken aback by his mother's frankness.

'I'm sure Uncle Fernandez has more than one guest room,' he said coolly. 'He loves to entertain.'

'He has two extra bedrooms,' Dona Ana smiled, 'but for the next month your aunt has a friend staying with her.'

'I don't think I'll go to Lisbon anyway,' Sharley intervened hastily.

'If you wish to come with me,' Marcos said, 'we can stay in an hotel.'

'Why don't you open up the town house?' his mother asked.

'It's too much trouble. Anyway, the sooner we sell it and put the money to good use, the better.'

'You're speaking like a Scotsman.'

'That should please you!'

His mother chuckled and Marcos gave a broad smile. It was unusual for him, and Sharley marvelled at the change which humour brought to his face: he looked carefree and young and far less foreign. But even as she watched him, the smile vanished and he was his dour self again.

'I've put a car at your disposal, Charlotte,' he suddenly announced, his long, slim fingers crumpling his napkin. 'I meant to tell you earlier, but it slipped my mind. However, if you prefer it, the chauffeur can drive you.'

'I enjoy driving myself,' she said quickly. 'Will it be all right if I go to Oporto?'

'Of course. But be careful of the traffic.'

They left the dinner table and returned to the *sala*, though Marcos soon excused himself to do some paper work.

'I shall be leaving first thing in the morning,' he said from the doorway, 'so I won't be seeing you before I go.'

'Have a safe journey,' his mother counselled.

'Be good,' Sharley said, straight-faced.

'I am always good. Sometimes even exemplary.'

Sharley grinned, and Marcos acknowledged it with a lift of one dark eyebrow, before departing.

'I feel I prevented you from going to Lisbon with Marcos,' Dora Ana said impulsively. 'I should have kept quiet.'

'Oh no,' Sharley protested. 'It would have been extremely awkward if I'd gone with him. I'd never share a ...' She drew a deep breath. 'Does your brother-in-law know the true circumstances of our marriage?'

'No one knows. Marcos believes—and I agree—that the fewer people who know, the better.'

'Pedro Lopez and the man who took the photographs know it's a sham.'

'We realise that. But apart from those two, and the small group with whom they work, no one else is aware of it. And as long as you are my son's wife, those despicable photographs have no scandal value.' Dona Ana rose and walked restlessly round the room. 'If only Marcos would give this up and settle in Scotland. He has so much to be proud of there.'

'I can't see your son as a Scotsman,' Sharley commented with amusement. 'He's a typical Portuguese.'

'Do you know many?'

'No, but——' Sharley coloured. 'That was a silly remark for me to make. What I meant was that he's typical of—of ...'

'Typical of all intelligent, good-looking young men. With enough personality to intrigue you, and enough arrogance to make you want to bring them to heel!'

Sharley gasped, and Dona Ana chuckled.

'I know exactly how exasperated Marcos can make you feel, my dear. I felt exactly the same way about his father when I first met him.'

'Were they alike?'

'Very much so. That's why when I first saw you ...' The hazel eyes regarded her reflectively. 'It would be lovely if your marriage became a real one.'

'There's no chance of that,' Sharley assured her.

'How can you be sure?'

'Because your son and I don't happen to be in love with each other.'

'But he's attracted to you.'

'No more than he would be to any other presentable-looking female.'

'Much more,' Dona Ana disagreed. 'You make him angry. That's how I guessed he's not as immune to you as you think.'

'I don't see how you can construe anger as a liking for me!'

'It's simple, my dear. If you meant nothing to him, you wouldn't arouse his anger sufficiently for him to care.'

'He *doesn't* care,' Sharley repeated formally. 'He's only interested in me for business reasons.' Forestalling any reply—for she did not relish further discussion of Marcos' feelings or her own—she rose. 'It's late, Dona Ana. If you'll excuse me, I'd like to go to my room.'

As she lay in bed, Sharley mulled over the evening's conversation. It would be unwise to disregard what her mother-in-law had said. After all, Marcos had kissed her—and passionately too—in the vineyard. But she was certain his interest in her only stemmed from pique. She had not been easy to win over—impervious both to his looks and position—and he had been forced to bring pressure to bear, via her godfather, before she agreed to marry him.

She could imagine how shattering such indifference must have been to a man so used to female adulation, and to add further insult to injury, she had made it clear from the moment she arrived here that she was counting the days until they could part.

Sitting up in bed—she was too restless to sleep—she hugged her knees and pondered on the state of her emotions. There was no doubt they were in a turmoil. Her desire to return to England stemmed from far more than an urge to resume her career. If she were honest, she would admit she could be equally happy with any other occupation connected with writing, and if she spent a year in Portugal, she might even achieve one of her greatest ambitions and write a novel.

So why was she so eager to leave? With a deep sigh she acknowledged that it was Marcos from whom she wanted to run away. He was going to be a difficult man to forget, and the longer she was with him, the longer he would disturb her peace of mind after they parted.

But was it peace of mind she wanted? What about adventure and fun? Even romance? Somehow she could not imagine herself having a lighthearted relationship with the aloof man whose ring she wore. Nor a deep one either, she told herself quickly. Marcos was not her type.

Deliberately she thought about him. She had never been in love, yet she was certain that when the right man came along she would know it immediately.

And it could never be someone like Marcos Santana. Or could it?

Her irrational dislike of him suggested that subconsciously she was afraid of this very thing happening, and was trying to build up an antipathy towards him as a form of self-protection.

Nervous at where her thoughts were taking her, she threw aside the coverlet and padded over to the window. The vineyards were bathed in moonlight and deep peace enveloped the countryside. This was Marcos' inheritance and she could not blame him for fighting to preserve it. She opened the window wider and leaned her elbows on the sill. The air was still and warm, and only the slightest rustle of a breeze disturbed the trees and broke the silence.

Suddenly Sharley noticed a light in the patio beneath her, and heard footsteps moving along it. She peered into the darkness and a shape took form. Marcos' shape; tall and proud.

'Why aren't you asleep, Charlotte?' His soft, mellifluous voice wafted up to her and she gave a start of surprise.

'How did you know I wasn't?'

'I heard your window open and I can see you in your nightdress.'

Hastily, Sharley drew back a little. 'You shouldn't be looking.'

'I can only see a pale blur. But I'm glad you don't wear pyjamas.'

Sharley knew Marcos was flirting with her again—he really did resent her indifference to him—and could not resist a provocative retort.

'I'm glad to see you're interested in women, *senhor*. I was beginning to wonder if you were totally celibate.'

'Didn't my kisses the other night disprove such a thought?' he asked sardonically.

'They proved you capable of passion. But the savage way you released it showed me you usually keep your feelings tightly leashed—the way a celibate might.'

'I'm no celibate,' he said flatly. 'Nor am I always so savage. But you angered me and I lost my temper. However, I'm more than willing to show you how gentle I can be.'

'No, thanks,' Sharley said quickly. 'I'll take your word for it.'

'I don't know why you harbour such strange ideas about me,' he went on, half to himself. '*You* weren't married either, when we first met, yet I never assumed you had aspirations to be a nun!'

'*I've* never been in love,' she replied. 'But you——' She stopped and went to move away from the window.

'Don't go,' he called sharply. 'Please finish what you were saying.'

She hesitated, reluctant to put her thoughts into words, and wishing she had been more careful to guard her way-ward tongue.

'Go on,' he repeated. 'Tell me what you were going to say.'

'I was going to remind you of your obligations to Teresa.'

For fully a moment he did not reply. Sharley waited, tense and curious, knowing that since he had demanded to know what was in her mind, he was obligated to make some comment on it.

'I've been considering marriage for more than a year,' he said finally. 'I owe it to my position—to my inheritance—to continue the family line. I had thought of marrying Teresa—it's obvious that I should, considering I know her so well—but I hadn't made up my mind. And now, of course, I can't think of it.'

'I don't see why. You won't be married to me for long.'

'So you keep reminding me.'

'Because it's true.'

Marcos moved a step closer, until he was directly beneath her window. He looked up at her, but his face was a pale blur and its expression was unreadable.

'Believe me, Charlotte, I want to end this pretence as much as you do. The moment it's feasible, we shall part.'

The quiet sincerity in his voice should have pleased her, but it had the opposite effect and, with a surprising sense of rejection, Sharley murmured 'goodnight' and withdrew into her room.

What's the matter with me? she asked herself as she lay in bed again. Why should I be upset because Marcos is as keen to end this phoney marriage as I am? The answer was obviously hurt pride, and she tried to rationalise it away. After all, he was merely being logical in his desire to have a normal marriage as quickly as he could, for only then could he have the heir he wanted. Yet he did not seem perturbed over who was going to be the mother

of his children; Teresa or some other Portuguese ar
crat.

That's why I'm so furious with him, Sharley admitted.
Because he makes the whole thing seem so practical and
unloving. Yet perhaps he was incapable of love. He could
feel passion—as she very well knew—but it looked as if
the deeper feelings of tenderness and caring, were beyond
him.

Upon which sobering thought, Sharley banged her
pillow with her fist, then burrowed into its feathery depths
to try to court sleep.

CHAPTER EIGHT

WITH Marcos gone, Sharley found the *quinta* lonely and alien, and it made her realise how much she missed his presence.

For the first two days she spent a great deal of time with Dona Ana, learning about the cultivation of the vines and the way the Santana Wine Company was run. Unlike many upper class Portuguese families, the Santanas had not invested their money in the Portuguese colonies, with the result that when these had become independent, the family had not suffered any financial loss.

'Our wealth doesn't depend on port wine,' Dona Ana said. 'If Pedro Lopez had been less impatient, and gone about things in the right way, Marcos would have made this company into a co-operative.'

'Rebels don't usually have patience,' Sharley sighed. 'I should know—I used to be one myself.'

'And now you're a sophisticated and charming young woman.'

'Not all that sophisticated,' Sharley grinned. 'And not so charming, either.'

Dona Ana's grey-green eyes twinkled. 'When Marcos told me that he planned to marry you, he described you as a cool blonde charmer.'

Sharley was astonished, but the older woman did not seem to notice and went on chatting.

'It's such a joy to have an Englishwoman here with me. If there's anything I can do to help you, please don't hesitate to ask. I've already told you how much I appreciate what you've done for my son. In the best of circumstances it would be difficult to marry a stranger, it must have been even harder for you to leave your h and friends and come to a foreign country.'

'Having a Scottish mother-in-law has been an unexpected help,' Sharley grinned. 'And I love this house and the beautiful countryside.'

'It's a pity you don't love my son as well.'

Sharley did not answer, but her expression made the older woman sigh.

'Forgive me, my dear. But hope dies hard.'

'Particularly a woman's,' Sharley replied, with a faint sigh. 'We're such obstinate creatures.'

Dressing for dinner that night, she took extra care with her appearance; perhaps she wanted to convey the impression to Dona Ana that even without Marcos' presence, she still liked to look her best.

Although no guests were staying at the *quinta*— Marcos having explained that as they were newlyweds, no one would expect them to entertain for several months—the life-style was still elaborate. The table was always impeccably set with exquisite linen and silver, no matter how simple the meal, and it was the custom to change for dinner. It was totally different from Sharley's casual life-style in England, and she thought how intrigued her women readers would be to know there were still parts of the world where traditional social conventions were maintained, despite the insecurity of the present day.

Perhaps it was this which made families like the Santanas cling so tightly to the heritage and the traditions of the past. But it was not only the façade which Dona Ana and her son preserved. They truly believed in the old-fashioned concept of 'noblesse oblige'; that being part of the nobility brought with it an obligation to behave honourably and generously towards those less privileged.

Dona Ana had told Sharley she hoped the political and social revolution which was now transforming Portugal would not affect its moral and religious thinking. But Sharley feared otherwise. The new democratic government would make Portugal a more egalitarian and prosperous country, but as the doors opened to the influences of the so-called 'advanced' Western states, materialism and selfishness and all the worst aspects of the twentieth century would slowly seep in.

The next day Sharley decided to go to Oporto. The car which Markos had put at her disposal was small and easy to drive. It was pleasant cruising along the narrow lanes; passing groups of peasants working in the fields and the occasional man on a bicycle; once a Ford Zodiac bearing the legendary 'GB' whizzed by her; but mainly she had the road to herself.

She had been driving for almost an hour when the scenery began to change. The miles of flat terrain covered by vineyards gave way to undulating countryside dotted with small villages. Then ahead of her on the horizon she saw the outline of tall factories and warehouses, and realised she must be approaching the outskirts of Oporto.

Expecting to see working-class blocks of flats as she entered the suburbs, she was surprised at the huddles of dilapidated old houses. These slums would be an eyesore in Britain, but beneath the blazing sun of Portugal they took on a certain picturesque, albeit doubtful charm.

Sharley drove along the east bank of the River Douro, and past one of the oldest districts of the city. To the south lay the red-tiled warehouses where port was blended and stored ready for shipment to all parts of the world. It was a busy, thriving area, and seventeen per cent of the country's population lived here. Soon she found herself in the centre of Oporto. The architecture was a mixture of Gothic and Baroque, with several examples of Arte Manuelina, a national style which had developed in the late sixteenth century, incorporating several forms of luxurious, ornamental decoration.

Parking her car—unlike in a city in England this was comparatively easy—Sharley set out to explore, glad she was wearing flat-heeled shoes.

As always in Latin countries, the older women were dressed predominantly in black. But the young girls wore bright colours, looking for all the world like butterflies as they strolled along the wide boulevards and through the narrow, cobbled byways. Soon Sharley neared the harbour. Fish restaurants abounded here; simple places with small round wooden tables bedecked with plain coloured cloths, where rough red wine was served in thick glasses, and the fish was so fresh it barely needed cooking.

Sharley had had an early breakfast and by noon was more than ready for lunch, which she took in one of the prettiest of the cafés. She sat outside at a table in the sunshine, and because she was alone and obviously a foreigner, she was the centre of all eyes. She found it pleasant to watch the passing parade: dusky-skinned, dark-eyed young women and swarthy, hot-eyed young men; fat babies being carried in their mother's arms, and old men swapping confidences as they stood together in bunches or sat or strolled in the warm sun.

It was all so peaceful that Sharley was tempted to stay here for the rest of the day. But she had done hardly any sightseeing, and she rose reluctantly, paid her bill and set off once again.

The shops were still closed for lunch and the siesta, and she window-shopped instead. She could not help noticing that though she was in the fashionable area, there were hardly any dress shops to be seen. The few she did discover were very small and displayed only one or two garments in the window. She wondered about this, until she remembered that Portugal, like Spain, was the home of the little dressmaker. Armed with your favourite fashion magazine and a bolt of material, you could have an exact copy of a Paris or Rome model made personally for you; hence the lack of demand for off-the-peg clothes.

Sharley noticed a large drapery shop, its windows filled with fabrics and dressmaking accessories. The owner was unlocking the door and, noticing her interest, smiled at her welcomingly, stepping back and waving his arm to usher her in. Sharley had brought very little money with her and wasn't able to buy anything, but she feasted her eyes on the bolts of magnificent brocades and silks.

'You wish buy?' the owner of the shop asked in halting English. 'We change dollars.'

Sharley smiled and shook her head. 'I'm not American.'

Leaving the shop eventually, she made her way slowly to her car, her thoughts unexpectedly turning to Marcos, wondering what he was doing in Lisbon. A sharp exclamation from behind her made her stop, and she stiffened as someone grasped her by the shoulders.

'Sharley ? *Por amor de Deus!* What are you doing in Oporto? How long have you been here? How long are you staying?'

Sharley swung round, astonished to see an old school friend of hers. Happily the two girls clasped one another.

'I didn't know you were in Oporto, Luisa. The last time I heard, you were working in New York.'

'I came back two months ago. I wasn't happy about it, but Pedro—my brother—needed me.'

A troubled expression crossed the girl's narrow, dark face, but it was gone as quickly as it came, banished by a wide smile which showed perfect white teeth, and made her look far less sulky than most Portuguese girls.

A passer-by jostled them, apologising, and Luisa caught Sharley's arm. 'Let's have a coffee. We can't talk here, and I have so much to tell you.'

'So have I,' Sharley said, and then hesitated, knowing she dared not disclose the true position between herself and Marcos. The thought of having to lie to an old school friend of whom she had always been fond—although they had rarely met since leaving boarding school—robbed her of the pleasure she would normally have felt at meeting her so unexpectedly.

They stopped at an open-air café and Luisa dumped her bag and shopping beside a table in the shade. Then she sat down and tilted her head expectantly as she waited for Sharley to tell her what she was doing here.

'I've been in Portugal several weeks,' Sharley began. 'Actually I—I'm married. I'm here with my husband.'

'But that's wonderful! I had a letter from Caroline three weeks ago,' Luisa referred to a mutual old school friend whom Sharley saw frequently in London, 'but she never said a word about you being married.'

'I wasn't, at the time. It was all—the whole thing was very sudden. Love at first sight, you might say—and a whirlwind courtship.'

'How romantic!' Luisa's dark eyes sparkled. 'Is that why you're looking so beautiful? Even in a gymslip you always looked like a model.'

'What an exaggeration!' Sharley giggled. 'I remember being fat and spotty and as untidy as you were.'

'That's not true,' Luisa giggled back. 'But let's forget the past. It's the *present* I want to know about. What's your husband like? Who is he? What does he do? Is he in Portugal on business? Do you have a picture of him?'

'Hey, hang on!' Sharley protested.

'That's what my brother always says. He calls me a firecracker because I'm always going off in different directions.' Luisa folded her hands together and clasped them firmly in her lap, as if to control her excitement. 'Tell me everything, Sharley. I want to know all the wonderful, romantic details.'

'Not all,' Sharley teased, deciding it would be easier if she played things lightly. 'My husband is Portuguese and we live outside Oporto.'

'Portuguese? But that's fantastic. Then we're neighbours.'

'Not really. I live on a wine estate about an hour away.'

'It's all sounding more and more intriguing. How long have you been here?'

'Since I was married—almost three weeks ago.'

'Then you're still very much a bride.' Luise glanced round as if expecting to see Sharley's husband. 'Why are you on your own?'

'My husband had to go to Lisbon.'

'And you stayed behind?'

'He went on business. We wouldn't have had much time to be together.'

'Poor you,' Luisa commiserated. 'When will he be back?'

'At the end of the week.'

'So you're free until then? That's wonderful. You must come and stay with me. We'll go back to your home to collect some of your things and——'

'I can't do that,' Sharley interrupted. 'Dona Ana wouldn't like it. My mother-in-law,' she explained, seeing her friend's questioning look. 'She'd think it strange if I left the house and stayed away, even for a night.'

'I can't see why,' said Luisa. 'Just explain that we're old school friends and that I've invited you over for a few days.'

'I really couldn't, Luisa. At least not for the moment. But I'd love to come home with you for dinner. I'll telephone my mother-in-law and tell her not to expect me until late.'

As if realising there was no point insisting, Luisa nodded and, forgetting completely about the coffee she had suggested, rose to hail a passing taxi.

'There's no need for that.' Sharley caught her friend's arm and propelled her across the road to her parked car.

Luisa regarded its sleek lines with admiration. 'Wow! Is this your husband's? He must truly love you if he lets you drive it. A man and his sports car are usually not to be separated.'

'My husband doesn't use this one. He has his own.'

'Better and better, my dear Charlotte.' Luisa aped the voice of their former headmistress. 'You have made an excellent match, my child. Quite worthy of one of my girls.'

Sharley collapsed into laughter. Mrs Derwent had always been delighted when a former pupil made a good marriage; 'good', according to her, being someone who was a member of the aristocracy or extremely rich.

'I refuse to believe you married for money,' Luisa went on. 'So you've obviously been lucky enough to fall in love with a rich man.'

Deciding it was wiser not to pursue the subject, Sharley changed it. 'Tell me about yourself. It's more than two years since I've seen you. Just after you lost your parents.'

'My life changed completely after that.' Luisa was suddenly serious. 'The estate was left in a dreadful mess and my brother wasn't able to sort things out. That's one of the reasons I came back here. But we've finally managed to settle things and we're not too badly off. We have a small income and a large house which we share with friends—so that at least pays for its upkeep.'

'What does your brother do?'

'He has many interests. He taught at university for a while, but he found it difficult to settle down. He didn't enjoy the academic life. I guess he's more of a doer than a talker, and he likes putting his ideas into action.'

'I can understand that,' said Sharley. 'By deeds, not words . . .'

'You'll be needing words from me now,' Luisa smiled, and gave Sharley directions.

Soon they were in a quieter, older section of the city and, turning into a cobbled roadway, stopped outside a tall, narrow house. The front door was painted black, and black railings edged the narrow balconies that marked the shuttered windows. From the topmost balcony a shirt hung, flapping in the slight breeze.

'That Juan!' Luisa muttered. 'He does his own washing and he's too lazy to go down and hang his things on the line in the garden. He's one of our friends,' she added.

'How many of you live here?'

'It varies. Sometimes we're eight or nine. There have even been twelve on occasions. We keep open house.'

'It sounds like a hippy commune.'

'It's nothing like that,' Luisa protested, unlocking the door and beckoning to her friend to enter.

Sharley found herself in a small, stone-walled hall, with a narrow but graceful staircase winding up to the first floor.

'I think everyone's in the kitchen,' said Luisa, and led Sharley to a room at the back of the house.

The kitchen seemed overflowing with serious-looking young men. They were all olive-skinned with black hair, and were in sombre shirts and sweaters. They smiled a greeting as they were introduced to Sharley, and a slim, medium-built young man rose from their midst and came

over to them. Sharley guessed, from the strong resemblance to Luisa, that it was her brother.

He looked puzzled as he shook Sharley's hand. 'Don't I
know you from somewhere?' he began, then quickly
added: 'No, that's impossible.'

'Don't you remember me speaking about Sharley when
I was at school in England?' Luisa intervened. 'She was
one of my best friends.'

'Of course.' Luisa's brother nodded, and the puzzled
expression gave way to a relaxed smile. 'My sister's letters
were full of you, and I used to wonder at your unusal
name.' He looked at Luisa. 'Pour some coffee for our
guest. Or would you prefer some wine?' he enquired.

'I'll have some coffee, please,' Sharley smiled.

The young man straddled a chair beside her with an
ease and grace that spoke of well co-ordinated muscles.
She noticed that all the young men seemed to have the
same litheness of movement, though most of them were
coarser featured than Luisa's brother.

'I hope I'm not intruding,' Sharley said.

'Not at all. We're having one of our conferences. But as
we have four or five a day, your interruption doesn't
matter.'

'Four or five a *day*?' she questioned. 'What do you find
to talk about?'

'A great many things. Big changes have taken place in
our country, as you may know.'

'I certainly do. News is my business. Until I married, I
was a journalist on a London paper—the *Weekly News*.'

The young man looked interested. 'It's a pity you no
longer work for them. We would like the British public to
know what's going on here.'

'Please don't talk politics,' Luisa said sharply. 'Sharley
is a visitor.'

'But once a reporter, always a reporter,' Luisa's brother

admonished, giving Sharley a keen glance. 'I'm sure you're interested in what's going on here.'

'Sharley's more interested in her personal life,' Luisa quipped. 'She's just married a Portuguese.' Setting the coffee tray on the table, she passed round the cups, then raised hers in her friend's direction. 'To your happy marriage and to your lucky husband—whoever he is,' she teased. 'Do you know, you still haven't told me his name.'

'It's Marcos,' Sharley said. 'Marcos Santana.'

There was a deathly silence, broken only by Luisa's cup clattering to the floor.

'Marcos Santana?' Luisa's brother exclaimed, his face pale. 'He is your *husband*?'

'Yes.' Sharley was surprised by the reaction Marcos' name had caused. 'Do you know him?'

'Yes.' Dark eyes raked her face. 'So that's why I thought I recognised you . . . The wedding pictures in the papers,' he added hastily, then gave her an intent look. 'Has he not mentioned my name to you?'

Sharley gave him a faint smile. 'I'm afraid I don't know it—Luisa hasn't told me.'

'Then we must remedy the situation.' He straightened. 'I am Pedro Lopez.'

It took an instant for the name to register, but as it did, the blood drained from Sharley's face, returning with a rush that made her ears throb. Luisa Lopez. Pedro Lopez. Idiot that she was! It had never occurred to her to connect the notorious Pedro with her old school friend; Lopez was such a common family name in Portugal.

'It is obvious my name is not unknown to you,' Pedro went on. 'I am sorry if Luisa brought you here under false pretences.'

'There was no pretence,' Luisa intervened quickly. 'I didn't know the name of Sharley's husband until now. All I knew was that he lived outside Oporto on a wine estate and . . . and . . . Oh, Sharley, how could you have married such a man?'

Sharley looked at her friend. Recalling the embarrassing and degrading episode of the photographs taken of herself and Marcos, she almost flung away the coffee cup she was holding.

'I presume this hasn't also been drugged?' she asked in a hard voice.

Luisa's eyelids fluttered, and a deep flush stained her face.

'Luisa had nothing to do with the taking of the pictures,' Pedro said. 'We did not discuss it with her, and she never saw them.'

Sharley did not doubt Pedro's words, and immediately regretted her angry accusation. She touched Luisa's shoulder in a placatory gesture and the girl responded by catching hold of her hand.

'I think I should leave,' Sharley murmured.

'You needn't be afraid to stay here.' Pedro's voice stopped her as she moved towards the door. 'You are quite safe with us.'

'You mean you have no further schemes hidden up your sleeve to humiliate my husband?'

How easily the word 'husband' came to her lips. Somehow Sharley felt very close to Marcos at this moment: as if in defending him she had drawn closer to him.

'Pedro knew nothing about the photographs either,' Luisa said in a rush. 'He was as surprised as——'

'Be quiet!' her brother said impatiently. 'Sharley isn't interested in explanations.'

'Yes, I am. I want the truth.'

Luisa turned to her brother. 'Tell her it wasn't your idea. Admit that it was Alvarez. You tried to stop him, but he——'

'Be quiet!' Pedro hissed, keeping his voice low. 'Alvarez is our ally. That's all that concerns Santana and his wife.'

Though the other men in the kitchen did not understand the conversation, they had looked up when the names Marcos Santana and Alvarez had been mentioned, and Pedro, sensing their growing curiosity, spoke to them in Portuguese before swinging back to Sharley.

'It's better if we continue our talk in another room.'

'We have nothing to talk about,' said Sharley. 'I'm leaving.'

'You can't go in anger,' Luisa cried, tears filling her eyes. 'Please, Sharley, you're my friend. Stay and talk to Pedro.'

'No,' Pedro cut in, giving Sharley a look of scorn. 'Don't stay because you're a friend of my sister's. If that's your only reason, then it's better if you go. But if you do stay, it should be because you once worked for a reputable newspaper, and you still care about the truth.'

'Truth can be distorted,' Sharley flared. 'As you very well know. But if it will appease your conscience to tell me your side of the dispute, then I'll listen.'

Silently Pedro led the way into the living room. It was simply furnished with a table, high-backed wooden chairs and hard spring settee, on which Sharley took a seat beside Luisa, while Pedro sat at the table.

'We wished to find a lever we could use against Santana,' he began, his dark eyes meeting hers briefly before sliding away. 'Our negotiations with him weren't getting us anywhere. He was too rigid and he wanted things done in his own time.'

'He was willing to come to terms with you,' Sharley corrected coldly. 'He was prepared to form a co-operative with the men, but he needed time to work things out.'

'Time?' Pedro almost spat out the word. 'Stalling; that's what he was doing. Hoping that if he prevaricated long enough, we'd lose face with the men; that would have given him the opportunity to talk them round to his own way of thinking.'

'That's a lie! My husband agreed to do as you wanted, and he would never have gone back on his word.'

Pedro gave an exclamation of anger, but before he could reply properly, the door was flung open and a short, stockily built man strode in. He was in his late thirties, with greying hair and belligerent, bulbous features. Instinctively Sharley knew this was Alvarez. Her stomach muscles tensed and she was filled with disgust, but with an effort she retained her control and kept her face expressionless. The man said something in a low voice to Pedro, who rose and followed him out.

Sharley looked at Luisa. 'It's a waste of time for me to talk to your brother. He has a completely different view of Marcos, and I'm not prepared to argue with him.'

'At least don't blame him for those photographs,' Luisa pleaded. 'He had no idea Alvarez was planning to do such a thing.'

'Didn't he know Alvarez had gone to England for that very reason?'

'No. Alvarez said he was following Marcos Santana to London to try to find out more about his financial dealings there. Even when Alvarez showed him the pictures, he didn't explain how he had obtained them. He led Pedro to believe they were genuine.'

'Genuine?' Sharley was furious. 'Weren't you told we'd been drugged? That I'd only met Marcos that same afternoon?'

'No, we weren't told a thing—I swear it. Alvarez said that—that Marcos Santana had a woman in his apartment and was making love to her day and night, and not giving a thought to his company or the men who worked for him.'

Anger made it impossible for Sharley to speak, and it was a long moment before she was in control of herself again. 'I think it was extremely stupid of your brother to believe Marcos would behave the way Alvarez said. Did he honestly think my husband was the sort of man to indulge in that sort of thing when he had so many other problems on his mind?'

'Men often *forget* their problems that way,' Luisa defended.

'Not Marcos,' Sharley said so positively that Luisa sighed.

'Oh, Sharley, why are we arguing? I know Alvarez was wrong to do what he did, but do you imagine any industrial battle is won without *some* dirty work? Pedro and Alvarez believe deeply in what they're fighting for. Have you ever thought about the thousands of men who've given their lives to the Santana company? Who were ill paid for years and had no say in the management? Don't you believe every man has the right to control his own destiny? To use the sweat of his brow for his own needs, instead of helping rich, idle capitalists accumulate even larger fortunes?'

'Since when are all capitalists idle and rich?' Sharley said contemptuously. 'A capitalist is someone who believes in working to acquire capital and possessions. With taxes the way they are, far fewer people are inheriting their money. Many who are rich today, were the poor of yesterday. Besides, not every person is cut out to be a great earner or a boss. Even in the animal world there's a hierarchy. As for the Santana Company, I can assure you most of the workers are happy and have far greater freedom under Marcos than they would have if the company were controlled by power-hungry men like your brother and Alvarez.'

'How much do you know about the Santana Company,

except what you read in your British press?' Luisa demanded. 'You've been in Portugal for three weeks. Have you bothered to set foot inside any of your husband's factories?'

'I know that most of Marcos' workers *wanted* the merger with Fawcett and Lloyd. They're sensible enough to realise that Portuguese business needs foreign capital if standards of living are to rise in this country. So where would your brother and his fellow revolutionaries go for the capital *they'd* need? To Russia?'

Luisa gave an exclamation of annoyance. 'It's a waste of time arguing with you. You honestly believe your husband is right.'

'You can say that again. I wouldn't have married him otherwise.'

'And because of your belief you tied yourself to a man you barely knew?'

'I don't wish to discuss it any further,' Sharley said sharply, wondering if her friend guessed that the marriage was one of expediency. But even if she did, there was nothing Pedro and Alvarez could do about it. As Marcos' wife, she had successfully prevented those appalling photographs from having any scandal value.

'I'm truly ashamed of Alvarez's behaviour over the photographs,' Luisa said huskily. 'But not of the ideals which prompted it.'

'Are you saying that the end justifies the means?'

'No, but——'

'But! When you can answer "no" without having to qualify it, I'll see you again. Until then, I'd rather we didn't meet.'

Turning on her heel, Sharley walked out of the room. No one was in the corridor and she let herself out of the house and drove away. She was unaware which direction she took, knowing only that she had to put as much distance as possible between herself and the occupants of that gloomy, brooding house.

Eventually she stopped the car and, looking about her, saw she was in a poorer section of the city. Old ladies dressed in traditional black, with scarves tied round their heads and carrying large straw baskets, passed her along the cobbled street. On a stool in a doorway opposite sat a rough-featured woman, bare ankles and arms crossed, her expressionless eyes watching her unkempt children playing barefoot in the street in front of her. A mongrel dog raced past chasing a cat, and almost scattered a small group of men standing talking together on the corner.

Normally Sharley would have been intrigued by her surroundings, but she was too emotionally exhausted for the scene about her to make any impression. Leaning back in her seat, she closed her eyes. Slowly her body ceased its trembling and she felt her control return.

Dusk had fallen when she at last sat up, switched on the ignition and slowly found her way out of the city and back on the road leading to the *quinta*. But it was not till she saw its lights twinkling in the distance that she was able to relax. She felt she was coming home; as if the vineyards about her were somehow her own. And in a way, of course, they were, for they belonged to Marcos.

And she was his wife—for as long as he needed her.

CHAPTER NINE

It was almost dark when Sharley pulled up at the front door of the *quinta*. Standing on the verandah was Dona Ana's personal maid, Isobel, who came hurrying towards her as she climbed out of the car, and told her Dona Ana was waiting to see her in her room.

Running up the stairs, Sharley wondered whether to say anything about her meeting with Luisa and Pedro; but on reflection, decided against it.

Her anger had abated and she had had time to think rationally. She felt now that she wanted to see them again and learn more about their political ideals; to discover why they should distrust Marcos when he had gone out of his way to concede to their wishes. True, he had taken his time doing it, but that was only because he had wished to make sure the changes would take place to the best advantage of the company. Yet even as she considered another meeting with Pedro and Luisa, she knew how unwise it would be. As Marcos' wife she dared not put herself in a situation where her loyalty to him could be questioned.

She reached Dona Ana's room, knocked on the door and went in. It was the first time she had been in here, and her eyes widened with pleasure as she took in the simple furniture—so different from the ornate carved pieces which abounded elsewhere in the *quinta*; English designed antiques of the Regency and Georgian period; gold-framed watercolours on blue silk walls, and underfoot an Aubusson carpet, its muted pastel colours far more soothing to the eye than the vivid Portuguese rugs. The room was filled with flowers, in Royal Doulton vases and Wedgwood bowls; and Dresden figurines stood among the many personal possessions on the dressing-table and bed-side tables.

All this Sharley took in within a few seconds of entering, but then her attention was drawn to the woman in an armchair by the window. Her face was pale and her eyes worried.

'Is anything wrong, Dona Ana?' she asked.

'No, my dear, not now that you're safely back. But I was worried when you hadn't returned by four o'clock.'

Sharley bit her lip. She had completely forgotten to let her mother-in-law know she would be out late. But going to Luisa's home, and then driving aimlessly round the city, had delayed her return to well beyond the time she had expected to be back.

'I'm sorry,' she apologised. 'But I hadn't said what time I'd be back, and I didn't realise you would worry.'

'It was only because I couldn't imagine what was keeping you away so long. Oporto isn't my favourite city.'

'It has some interesting museums,' Sharley ventured, hoping Dona Ana would think she had paid them a visit. 'And I also found a lovely shop selling brocades and silks.' Quickly she went into a detailed description of the store and its owner.

'Aren't you going to show me what you bought?'

'Not a thing, unfortunately,' Sharley smiled. 'I didn't have enough money. But it was fun just browsing.'

Dona Ana frowned. 'Next time you go to Oporto you must ask Marcos for some Portuguese currency. He wouldn't like to think of you wandering penniless round the city.'

Sharley shrugged. She did not like the idea of taking money from Marcos, but did not wish to indicate this to his mother. Murmuring that she was going to have a rest before dinner, she went to her room. The nervous strain of the past few hours had exhausted her and she fell asleep as soon as she lay down, not wakening till past eight o'clock.

Refreshed by a quick shower, she ran lightly down to the *sala*. Her hair was still slightly damp and she had brushed it back from her face, which accentuated her delicate features and drew attention to her large, limpid eyes. She wore no make-up—which made her look even younger—and was dressed informally in a long flowered cotton skirt and pale blue blouse, a wide belt clasping her waist and emphasising its narrowness.

As she entered the *sala* a tall, jet-haired man turned from the mantelpiece and her heart skipped a beat.

'Marcos!' There was surprise in her voice. 'I didn't expect you till the end of the week.'

He eyed her appraisingly. 'I finished my business earlier than I anticipated and there was nothing to keep me in Lisbon.'

'I imagined you spending your spare time squiring some beautiful young lady,' she said lightly.

'Then you obviously haven't given thought to the wagging tongues of the society matrons. Can you imagine what they'd say if a bridegroom of a few weeks was seen in the company of another woman?'

Sharley said nothing, realising what a silly comment she had made. But Marcos refused to let the matter rest.

'It's important that we both keep up this pretence, Charlotte. We married for a specific reason, which still exists.'

'For how long?'

'Until the merger between your uncle's company and mine has been so effectively integrated that it cannot be undone.' Marcos' expression was as hard as his voice. 'But you know this already, so why the question? Do you think

I want to continue this farce for a moment longer than necessary?'

'Of course I don't!'

'Good. Then at least on one point, we understand one another.' He sipped at the drink he was holding, then suddenly set down his glass and went to the cabinet. He poured a glass of pale green sparkling wine and came over to her with it. 'One of our specialities,' he explained, his voice normal, polite. '*Vinho verde*. We are proud of the fact that ours beats that of all other competitors.'

Sharley sipped the wine and had to agree it was excellent. It was not too sweet and at the same time was not as dry as vintage champagne.

'What have you been doing in my absence?' he asked. 'I understand you were in Oporto today.'

'Yes. I felt like a drive and it was an opportunity to try out the car. It goes like a bird.'

'What do you think of the city?'

'I didn't do much exploring. I just felt like wondering about the streets and shops to absorb the atmosphere of the place.'

They both turned as Dona Ana, accompanied by Teresa, entered the room. Sharley had not expected to see the Portuguese girl here tonight, and was irritated at how lovely she looked. She was in a red dress of some diaphanous material, the bodice clearly indicating her well-shaped breasts and softly-curving shoulders; the creamy skin enhanced by a narrow circlet of diamonds at her throat. Sharley wore no jewellery and was conscious of how dowdy she must look next to Teresa. But at least she was tall and slender, and had the blonde looks that appealed to men of Latin race. Not that I want to, she thought, and tossed her head unconsciously. As she did, she caught Marcos eyeing her with barely concealed amusement. Damn him! He knew exactly what was going through her head.

At dinner, Teresa spoke mainly to Marcos, resisting all his attempts to make her speak English. Sharley found the girl's behaviour boorish, and knew it was being done deliberately to make her feel an outsider. Yet what did it matter? These people meant nothing to her; nothing whatever. Even as she thought this, Sharley knew she was lying to herself, and that in the space of a few weeks she had come to care very much for Dona Ana and this wonderful house. She even enjoyed her fights with Marcos.

'I saw you in Oporto today.' Teresa's voice, unexpectedly addressed to Sharley, interrupted her reverie. 'I was driving with Pae to his office, and saw you leaving Pedro Lopez' house.'

Sharley was too shocked to answer. Her eyes flew swiftly to Marcos' face and she saw that the shock had been equally great for him. But he was far quicker to recover than she, and he looked at Teresa scornfully.

'Lopez? That's impossible, Teresa. You were mistaken. Charlotte doesn't know him.'

'I was not mistaken, Marcos. Your wife's colouring makes her easily distinguishable.'

He looked directly at Sharley. 'Is this true?'

Aware of the guilty colour staining her cheeks, Sharley nodded. 'Pedro's sister Luisa was at school with me. We—er—bumped into each other in Oporto. I had no idea she was living there. She invited me back to her home and I—I met her brother there. It wasn't until he . . . until we started to talk that I realised who he was.'

'But you knew the name Pedro Lopez?' Marcos stated, his voice soft, though his eyes were hard as agates.

'There must be thousands of people with the name Lopez in Portugal,' Sharley answered as lightly as she could. After all, why should she feel guilty for an accident of fate? She had not expected to bump into Luisa, and would not have visited her home had she known who she would meet there. 'Luisa never told me her brother's first name, but even if she had, I doubt if I'd have connected the two. It was only when I actually saw him with his friends—accomplices, I suppose—that I realised who he was.'

'It must have been very embarrassing for you,' Dona Ana said sympathetically, coming quickly into the conversation.

'It was.' Sharley flung her mother-in-law a grateful look. 'Especially when they discovered I was married to Marcos. That was a dreadful moment. I had the feeling they wanted to lynch me.'

'*Por amor de Deus!*' Marcos exclaimed angrily. 'How dare those scoundrels frighten you!'

Sharley hid her surprise that he should be concerned by this.

'They didn't harm me,' she placated. 'The whole thing was an unfortunate incident that I'd like to forget.'

'Men like Lopez can never be forgotten,' Marcos stormed. 'Even when they are defeated they refuse to concede victory to their opponents.' He drew a deep breath, as if trying to calm himself. 'Now you know who your friend's brother is, I trust you will not see either of them again.'

Marcos' high-handed assumption that she would do as he ordered put Sharley on the defensive. Although only moments ago, she had not had any intention of seeing Luisa again, now she was not so sure.

'It's going to be very awkward for me to ignore my friend. I've known her for years and I don't want to hurt her.'

'Your kindness does you credit, *amada*. Nevertheless I forbid you to see her.'

'Why? She isn't responsible for her brother.'

'She condones what he does. If she didn't, she wouldn't live with him.'

'She feels he needs her. Their parents are dead and she is all the family Pedro has.'

'I do not wish to discuss it any longer,' Marcos said coldly, his hand clenching around the stem of his glass in a way that made Sharley think he wished it were her throat.

'Everyone has a mind of their own,' she said tartly, 'though you often seem to forget it.'

'Your friend is living with my enemy. This means she isn't to be trusted.'

'I'm sure Charlotte is as concerned to safeguard the interests of the Santana Company as we are,' Dona Ana interrupted. 'She's your wife and knows where her duty lies. She knew it when she married you.'

Realising how true this was, Marcos had the grace to look abashed.

'Please forgive me, Charlotte,' he said. 'My concern for your welfare overcame my control. I know only too well that you are a loyal wife.'

Appreciating that the latter half of his apology was made for Teresa's benefit, Sharley gave a cool smile, but the unpleasant scene had ruined her appetite and she soon stopped even trying to eat.

She was relieved when the meal was over and they adjourned to the *sala*. Her only sense of satisfaction came from seeing Teresa's discomfiture at having failed to discredit her, and she was more than ever convinced that the girl was her enemy. It was not surprising, since her marriage to Marcos had put paid to Teresa's own hopes of becoming his wife. But only temporarily, did the girl but know it.

Although the religion of Portugal was predominently Catholic, Marcos would have no difficulty in obtaining an annulment. Recollecting his insistence that they have a civil ceremony only, Sharley knew he had made this decision to obviate any complications when the time came to gain his freedom. Unexpectedly she was depressed by the thought and tried to analyse it away, finally deciding it was not that she particularly cared whether Marcos married someone else once they had parted; what she disliked was the idea of it being to a rude, arrogant girl like Teresa.

Surreptitiously she glanced at Marcos. He sat quiet and relaxed in a tall-backed chair, his lean, tanned fingers resting on the ornately carved arms. She knew she meant nothing to him. Once she left his home he would not give her a second thought. She wondered if he would be surprised to know that she herself would find it extremely difficult to forget him. It was a disquieting admission.

As if aware of what was going through her mind, he lifted his head and their eyes met. Sharley felt a shiver go through her, almost as if he had touched her. The feeling excited her, yet left her with a sense of even greater disquiet.

Teresa stood up, the movement bringing her to Marcos' attention.

'Shall I take you home?' he asked at once.

'If you would be so kind.' Teresa smiled prettily as she bent to kiss Dona Ana farewell, then nodded coolly in Sharley's direction before she left the room.

A few moments later the still of the evening was broken by the purr of the car engine starting up and pulling away. Dona Ana picked up her sewing—a petit-point centre for a cushion—and for several moments there was silence. Then she put down her work and looked directly at Sharley.

'Why didn't you tell me you'd met an old school friend and her brother?' she asked quietly.

'There seemed little point. I had no intention of seeing

either of them again, and I didn't want to upset you.'

'I see.'

'There was another reason,' Sharley admitted. 'I was afraid you might think I'd had an ulterior motive.'

'An ulterior motive?'

'For seeing them. After all, it would make a fantastic scoop for my paper if I were able to do an in-depth interview with Pedro and Alvarez.'

'Such a thought never even occurred to me,' Dona Ana said without hesitation. 'Do you think that was why Teresa told us she had seen you?'

'Partly,' Sharley replied, throwing discretion to the wind. 'But her main intention was to discredit me in Marcos' eyes. She regards me as an interloper here, and quite frankly I don't blame her. If I were in her position I'd feel exactly the same.'

'Perhaps. But I don't think you would behave in the same way. Latin women can be far more tempestuous in the way they show their jealousy.' The dark head moved slightly. 'Teresa is undoubtedly fond of my son.'

'And extremely impressed by his position.'

'Is that his biggest recommendation?'

Realising she had been tactless, Sharley was embarrassed. 'No, of course not. He's attractive and intelligent and has a great deal of personal charm—when he wants to use it. I'm sure many women would give their eye teeth to marry him.'

'*All* their teeth,' Dona Ana chuckled. 'But Marcos can't be talked into doing anything he doesn't want. Simpering women, or those who show him how much they adore him, bore him to death. He's more attracted to someone who knows her own mind.'

'As long as her mind remains in tune with his,' Sharley replied bluntly. 'He might believe docile women don't appeal to him, but I can't see him being happy with——'

She almost said 'someone like me', but realising the implication, stopped herself in time.

However, Dona Ana had read her thoughts, and she smiled. 'You would be ideal for Marcos, Charlotte. You're intelligent, beautiful, well-bred and spirited.'

'I'm also independent and interested in having a career. It would never work, Dona Ana. Apart from which, Marcos and I don't love one another.'

'I know,' came the sigh. 'It was just a mother's dream. But I shall miss you when you leave us.'

'And I'll miss *you*,' said Sharley, and standing up, pleaded a headache as her reason for not waiting for Marcos' return. He was not going to come back from his tête-à-tête with Teresa to find his English wife waiting for him.

Tense and restless—her meeting with Luisa and Pedro had upset her more than she cared to admit—she decided to have a bath before going to bed.

The perfumed water was soft and warm on her skin, and she slid deep into it and tried to relax. But she found it impossible. As she dismissed Luisa from her mind, Teresa intruded. The girl had deliberately gone out of her way to make Sharley feel guilty tonight, and heaven knows what other ideas she might have put into Marcos' head. Then there was the added embarrassment of Dona Ana's affection. She hoped they would remain friends even after she left Portugal, but somehow she doubted it. She could not see herself returning here for a holiday once Teresa was installed as mistress. The very idea of it angered her all over again, and she jumped out of the bath and reached for a towelling robe.

Still not ready for sleep, she remained in the gown and curled up on the sofa at the foot of the bed. Idly she reached for something to read. It was a Portuguese fashion magazine and she leafed through the pages. But she could not concentrate, and after a while she returned to the bathroom and rubbed her hair dry, then brushed it until it hung in a silver-beige fall down her back. She changed into her nightdress, glimpsing her reflection in the mirrored wall. The champagne-coloured silk sinuously caressed her body and she slipped on a matching housecoat with long flowing sleeves. As she went into the bedroom, there was a knock on the door.

Her heart raced. 'Who is it?' she called.

'Marcos. I wish to speak to you. May I come in?'

Drawing a deep breath, Sharley opened the door a fraction.

'What is it, Marcos? It's late. Can't it wait until tomorrow?'

'If I felt it could,' he said drily, 'I wouldn't ask to talk to you now.'

Sharley made no attempt to move from the door and nor did he. Sighing, she stepped back.

'Very well. Come in if you must.'

He moved into the room and closed the door behind him. Dark eyes ranged slowly from her silky hair to the curves of her body. She resisted the urge to draw her housecoat closer around her and stepped farther away from him.

'Well, now you're here, what is it you want to say?'

'It isn't what *I* want to say. You are the one who has some explaining to do—about your meeting with Pedro Lopez.'

'I've nothing further to tell you about it. I was at school with Luisa and we bumped into each other in Oporto.'

'*Deus!* If the meeting was as innocent as you say, why were you afraid to tell me? Why did Teresa have to mention it first?'

'I was going to tell you—some time—but I wasn't sure how you would take it.'

'Why? What were you afraid of?'

'I wish you wouldn't try to make me feel guilty,' she protested. 'I assure you my meeting with Luisa was unpremeditated and innocent. If you can't understand why I was nervous of telling you about it, you must be very insensitive.'

'Perhaps you are *overly* sensitive,' he countered. 'I am surprised that an intelligent, articulate young woman like yourself could not be frank with me.'

Sharley silently agreed, though nothing would make her admit it.

'Teresa was right,' Marcos continued. 'That innocent look of yours hides a subtle and devious mind.'

'Unlike Teresa's, of course,' Sharley said scornfully.

'I haven't come here to talk about Teresa. It's Lopez I'm interested in.'

'Well, I'm not!' Sharley flared. 'I've never met him before in my life, and I know nothing about him.'

'But interviewing him would make an excllent story for your paper, wouldn't it?'

Anger robbed Sharley of words, and she stared at Marcos, speechless.

'Well?' he demanded. 'Why don't you defend yourself? Or will you admit that your meeting with him was pre-arranged?'

It was still impossible for Sharley to speak. Her face was pale and her breasts rose and fell in agitation. 'Please go,' she said finally, her voice low. 'We have nothing more to say to each other.'

'If anyone should go, it's you,' Marcos replied icily.

'That day can't come quickly enough,' Sharley retorted. 'I should never have allowed Uncle George to persuade me to marry you.'

'But since you did, you decided to take advantage of the situation to further your career.'

'That's not true!'

'Are you planning a series of articles for the *Weekly News*?' Marcos went on as if she had not spoken, 'or will you sell your story to the highest bidder in Fleet Street?'

For answer, Sharley picked up a pile of magazines and hurled them at him. The hard edge of one of them struck his cheek and he lifted his hand to his face. His eyes blazed with temper and he lunged forward and shook her violently by the shoulders.

'How dare you? No woman has ever lifted her hand to me!'

'There's always a first time!' Sharley shouted, struggling to free herself; but Marcos would not loosen his hold.

'What did Lopez say to you?' he demanded. 'Did he ask you to spy on me?'

'How dare you!'

Sharley beat her fists against Marcos' chest. His grip did not lessen and she began to sob.

'I hate you!' she cried. 'You deserve Teresa. You're two of a kind. The sooner you're free to marry her the better. The worst mistake I ever made was to become your wife!'

'I'm glad you've remembered you *are* my wife,' Marcos said forcefully, and pulling her hard against him, pressed his mouth on hers.

Sharley tried to struggle free, but the closeness of his body was her undoing. Tremors of desire flickered through her, weakening her resolve to resist him. She went limp in his hold and, aware of it, he eased his cruel grip on her.

'You madden me,' he said against her lips. 'When I'm with you I can't think straight.'

His hands moved over her body, as if hungry for the feel of her. Sharley felt the warmth of his fingers through the flimsy silk of her negligee, and the touch of the material seemed to arouse him to even stronger passion.

...nd his arms more tightly around her and pressed
...against the length of his body.

'You're a torment in my soul,' he said huskily. 'I love
you. I want you.'

'No!' she cried, and tried to slip from his arms. 'Let me
go!'

'Never! You're mine.'

The hardening of his body told her he wanted to make
it so, and though she longed to give in to him, she knew
that in the morning she would despise herself for it. What
Marcos called love, she could only call desire. He did not
trust her; he did not even like her, so how could anything
he felt for her be love?

'Don't keep fighting me,' he murmured passionately,
his mouth, trailing hot fire along the side of her neck and
down the curve of her breast. 'You want me, too. I can
feel it in the way you tremble; the way you respond to my
touch. Let me love you, *amada*.'

'Don't use the word love!' she cried. 'First you accuse
me of disloyalty and then you try to seduce me. If that's
your idea of love, you can keep it!'

As if her words were a whip, Marcos loosened his hold
on her. 'How quickly you berate me,' he said thickly.
'Doesn't being in my arms tell you anything more?'

'Sure it does. It tells me you're a passionate man who's
used to having his needs satisfied. But not by me,' she
added bitterly. 'Never by me. You believe Teresa's accusations, but you won't believe *my* side of the story. If you
really think I'm deceitful and career-mad, how can you
possibly love me? All you want is to possess me. And if
that's your idea of love, then give it to Teresa—or to any
other woman who takes your fancy!'

Marcos drew completely away from her. He was pale
but surprisingly composed, though the clenching of his
hands showed he was not unmoved by her accusations.

'You should guard your tongue,' he said quietly. 'One doesn't need a pneumatic drill to crack an eggshell.'

'You deserve everything I've said. You accuse me of being a scheming Mata Hari and then expect me to welcome you into my bed!'

'I doubt if you're woman enough to welcome *any* man there!'

'That's something you'll never find out,' she snapped. 'Now go, before either of us does anything else we might regret.'

'You need have no fear of that. What happened tonight will never be repeated.'

'That's the best news I've heard!'

Without another word Marcos swung out of the room. As the door closed behind him, Sharley collapsed on the bed and burst into tears. Her body was still aflame with desire and her mind was feverish with the sudden knowledge of how deeply she cared for him. But it would only be an ephemeral emotion, she kept telling herself as she tried to deny the sweeping longing that overcame her. How could one love a man yet at the same time dislike him so intensely? It put her feelings on a par with his; making it lust instead of love; a desire for physical satisfaction, for the pleasure of being possessed; for surrendering her body to the sensual passions he could arouse in her—as she could arouse in him.

As she remembered his cruel accusations, anger swiftly superseded all else. How could Marcos possibly believe she had only married him to obtain a scoop for her paper? It was such a monstrous accusation that her tears dried completely. She would not allow herself to love Marcos. It was a weakness of her body that her mind would have to control.

Pushing aside the coverlet, she slid between the sheets. Her limbs ached from the grip of his fingers on her flesh, and she tentatively touched her shoulders where he had held her so tightly. Though logic told her to despise him, she still yearned for his touch; for the feel of his mouth on hers, warm and searching as his hands. Once again tears flowed, and she buried her head in the pillow and cried herself to sleep.

When Sharley saw herself in the mirror next morning, she shuddered. Her eyes were red, her face puffy and her head throbbed. She had a cold wash, took some aspirins and went back to bed until her head stopped its pounding.

Only then did she get up and dress, making up carefully to disguise the telltale marks around her eyes. Then she went downstairs, hoping she looked as though she did not have a care in the world.

She was relieved to find the terrace empty, and she learned from the young maid who came out to serve her that Marcos had already had breakfast and left the *quinta*. Though Sharley had no appetite, she made herself eat one of the warm crisp rolls and some home-made jam. But the coffee was exceptionally welcome. Strong and aromatic, it stilled the nervous trembling of her hands, making her feel capable of coping with the day ahead.

She was pouring a second cup when her mother-in-law appeared. She looked worried, and for a brief moment Sharley was afraid her quarrel with Marcos had been overheard. But she relaxed when she remembered that the walls of the *quinta* were thick and that Dona Ana's rooms were at the opposite end of the house from her own.

'Where is Marcos?' his mother enquired. 'Has he gone out?'

'I think so. I haven't seen him this morning.'

Dona Ana moved across to the side of the terrace and leaned on the balustrade. Roses trailed around its pillars and behind her the garden was a riot of vivid colour, the air heady with the perfume from the flowers and shrubs.

'Marcos had a restless night,' Dona Ana murmured. 'I couldn't sleep myself, and at half past two, when I went to sit by my window, I saw him walking in the garden. I must have dozed off, and when I awoke again it was almost daylight, and he was still there.'

'It was a warm night,' said Sharley. 'I also found it difficult to sleep.'

'We're used to warm nights here,' Dona Ana replied. 'I'm certain Marcos' restlessness had nothing to do with the weather. It was your meeting with Pedro Lopez which upset him.'

'I'd rather we didn't talk about it,' Sharley said hastily.

'I wasn't implying anything, my dear. It was only my clumsy way of saying that Marcos may be wondering whether he's done everything possible to resolve the situation between himself and his employees.'

'It's too late for doubts. The merger's been concluded.'

'Even so, I——'

The telephone rang and they both paused as it was answered. Steps crossed the tiled floor and a maid appeared to tell Sharley there was a call for her. Anticipating who it might be, she went into the hall and picked up the receiver.

'Please don't be angry with me for ringing you,' said Luisa in a low voice, as if afraid of being overheard. 'But I *must* see you.'

'It's out of the question. It would be embarrassing for both of us.'

'But it's very important. It could affect both your husband and my brother.'

'I don't see how. There's nothing for us to discuss.'

'There is. Sharley, listen to me. I can't explain now—I'm in a public callbox and there are too many people about. But can you meet me at that café in Oporto this morning? Please, Sharley, I beg you to come!'

Luisa sounded so desperate that Sharley found it impossible to refuse. Reluctantly she agreed to meet her at noon, and before she had a chance for second thoughts, her friend replaced the receiver.

Returning to the terrace, Sharley found it deserted, and she went to her room and changed from slacks and blouse into a cream silk dress. She debated whether to tell her mother-in-law where she was going, then thought better of it. But on the way out she met the girl who had brought her breakfast and, speaking slowly in English, asked her to tell Dona Ana she was going for a drive and would not be in for lunch.

CHAPTER TEN

LUISA was waiting for Sharley at the café where they had gone to have coffee yesterday. It was a little more difficult to find a parking place for the car, and Sharley had to circle the crowded square twice before she found a spot, then hurried back to meet her friend.

'I'm so glad you came,' Luisa cried, catching her by the hand. 'I couldn't bear for us to part as we did, and I have to talk to you.'

'Let's order coffee first,' said Sharley, feeling in need of it. The knowledge that she was here against Marcos' wishes was unnerving her, and she felt surprisingly guilty.

Luisa sat quietly until their order came, then fiddling nervously with a spoon, began to talk.

'First I want to explain about my brother. He never intended the workers to gain control of the Santana Company. If it had been up to Pedro, he would have come to an agreement with Marcos—there's no question of it. But unfortunately Alvarez came on the scene. He's Cuban, as you know, and he's being financed by a militant group based outside Portugal, who are only interested in revolution. My brother didn't know this in the beginning. He thought Alvarez was a genuine idealist like himself—not a terrorist—and by the time he discovered the truth, it was too late.'

'Why?'

'Because Alvarez had brought in some of his own men and put himself in control.' Luisa sighed deeply. 'I saw through Alvarez long before my brother did. A woman's intuition rarely fails. But Pedro wouldn't listen to me. It's only now that he admits I was right.'

Sharley found her thoughts turning to Marcos. *Her* intuition hadn't been very successful where he was concerned. Look what a mistake she had made judging *his* character. With an effort she came back to what Luisa was saying.

'In the past few weeks—since those photographs were taken in fact—Pedro has realised how dangerous Alvarez really is. He wants to break away from him, but he's not sure how to go about it. Alvarez has many roughnecks supporting him and they'll use violence if necessary to keep him in control. I've heard rumours that they're planning to barricade themselves into one of your husband's textile factories.'

'Textile factories?' Sharley echoed in surprise.

'He doesn't only own vineyards, you know.'

'I didn't,' Sharley admitted wryly. 'I know very little about his business interests. I only married him to . . .' Her voice trailed away, but it was too late. Luisa's expression showed that she had guessed what had been left unsaid.

'You don't mean to tell me you only married Marcos Santana to prevent Alvarez using the photographs?' The dark eyes were full of amazement. 'Oh, Sharley, what made you do such a thing? You've ruined your whole life!'

'It wouldn't have done my life much good to have had those disgusting pictures flashed around the world. Reputable newspapers wouldn't have published them, but quite a few of the scandal sheets would. Libel laws aren't so strong in America or on the Continent, you know.'

This particular aspect of her position regarding the photographs had never occurred to her until now. She was also surprised it had not entered Marcos' mind either, for had it done, he would surely have used it as an argument at the very beginning, when he had been trying so hard to persuade her to marry him. Or had he been saving it as a last resort if she remained opposed to helping him? If this were the case, he had more of a heart than she realised.

'But do you love your husband now?' Luisa asked, bringing Sharley's attention back to the present.

'I'm very fond of him,' Sharley hedged. Marcos would be furious enough that Luisa had guessed the true reason for their marriage, without her also disclosing that she was counting the days for it to end.

'What a mess all this is!' Luisa was in tears. 'If only we could sort things out!'

'There's nothing to sort out,' Sharley said crisply. 'Pedro and Alvarez have lost their battle, though they'll never admit it. The Santana Wine Company has merged with my uncle's, and there's nothing anyone can do about it.'

'That's where you're wrong. The workers can still make trouble. Strikes—fights—many other things. And your husband knows it, even though he may not have said anything to you.'

Sharley frowned, sensing that what Luisa said was true. 'What do you propose, then? You said you wanted to talk to me, so I assume you've something in mind?'

'I have,' Luisa said earnestly. 'Pedro is sure that most of the men will listen to him if only he can get rid of Alvarez. But first, he asked me to find out from you whether you thought Marcos would agree to meet him again and re-open negotiations.'

'What sort of negotiations? I've already told you Marcos no longer has a free hand in the Santana Company.'

'But he still owns half of it,' Luisa said sharply. 'And he wants a contented work force, doesn't he, not a militant one?'

'Of course he does. But I thought your brother met Marcos in Oporto recently? Why didn't he talk to him about it then?'

'Because your husband was too angry to listen to what Pedro had to say. But he *must*. He has to realise that my brother has changed—that his sympathies lie far more with your husband than with Alvarez.'

'Marcos won't listen to me, Luisa. And why should he? Damn it all, he'll probably think it's another trick on your brother's part!'

'You'll have to convince him it isn't. And you can, Sharley. You married him to help him, didn't you? Surely he'll trust you? Talk to Pedro yourself, then you'll see how sincere he is. He's not a militant—he never was. All he wants is a decent standard for the workers.'

'So does Marcos. But your brother found him too slow in implementing any changes. So why should he think Marcos will be any different now?'

'He won't need to be,' Luisa stated. 'It's Pedro who's different. Sharley, I beg of you, help me. Try to get the two of them together.'

'I can't see it working.'

'It will. Look, if you've any doubts about Pedro, then see him again for yourself. Talk to him before you finally make up your mind. Once you've seen for yourself how sincere he is, I'm sure you won't have any doubts convincing your husband.'

'I can't meet your brother,' protested Sharley.

'Why not?'

Sharley hesitated, knowing how disloyal Marcos and Dona Ana would think her if she did as Luisa suggested. Yet somehow this wasn't the only reason for her reluctance. She had a strange premonition; of something momentous and unpleasant beginning to stir around her. But it was foolish to feel this way. There was no reason for her to be uneasy.

'Do it for *my* sake,' Luisa pleaded.

Once again Sharley found it impossible to ignore such a plea. 'Very well. But I can't stay long.'

Swiftly they drove to the house. It looked exactly the way it had done yesterday, even to the few garments flapping from the topmost balcony. Stifling her fear, Sharley followed Luisa inside. As they walked through the narrow hallway she heard voices from a room on their left, and the door was opened by Pedro. He gave them both a quick, half-embarrassed smile, then turned to murmur something to the people in the room before stepping forward and closing the door behind him.

'We will talk in the kitchen,' he said softly, and led the way down the hall.

The kitchen was empty, but a kettle was boiling on the stove, and Luisa made coffee while Pedro sat at the table with Sharley.

'Luisa has told me you wish to speak with my husband again,' she said.

'Yes. Will you arrange it for me?'

'I think you should approach Marcos yourself. He would have more respect for you if you did. Despite what you think, my—my husband is a reasonable man, and if you can persuade him that you've genuinely had a change of heart, I'm sure you'll be able to settle things between you. Asking me to plead with him on your behalf will only make matters worse.'

Pedro rubbed his hand reflectively along the side of his face. 'You may be right. In fact I think you are. You have much intelligence, *senhora*. I can see why Luisa is fond of you.' He smiled at her, and for the first time looked relaxed. 'I'm glad you came here today. I have been wanting to apologise to you for the embarrassment we caused you on your last visit.'

Sharley was about to reply when the door opened and Alvarez strode in. There was an air of repressed excitement about him which was apparent in the glazed look in his eyes and the twitching of his mouth. He's a brute, Sharley decided fearfully, and her earlier disquiet returned.

'I *thought* it was you,' said Alvarez in a heavy accent, glaring at her.

She glanced nervously at Luisa, who was looking equally uneasy. 'I promised Luisa I'd come back for another chat,' Sharley murmured, half rising from her chair. 'But I'm just going, as a matter of fact.'

'What's your hurry?' Alvarez' voice stopped her. 'Why don't you stay and have lunch with us? We cannot offer you the luxuries you would have at the Santana table, but we have grilled sardines and rough red wine.'

'That sounds delicious.' Sharley forced a smile to her lips. 'May I take a rain check on it? The family are expecting me back for lunch, and I don't want to disappoint them.'

'I'm sure they won't mind.'

Ignoring his comment, Sharley rose and headed for the door, stopping as she found Alvarez barring her way.

'Please, *senhor*. I'm sorry to decline your invitation, but I really can't stay. Another time, perhaps.'

'There'll be no other time.' The man's tone was menacing. 'You will stay.'

Sharley looked at Pedro and he came forward. But as he reached Alvarez, the older man pushed him aside with a sharp gesture.

'Sit down, Senhora Santana,' he said in a harsh voice. 'You are our guest and you will be staying here.'

'I don't think you heard me, *senhor*.'

'And you didn't hear *me*,' Alvarez mocked. 'You are not leaving.' He eyed Pedro. 'That goes for you and that sister of yours. I'm the one who gives orders here, no one else. Is that understood?'

'No, it isn't,' Pedro replied. 'You have no more right than anyone else. We represent the people and it is their wishes that count, not ours.'

Alvarez spat out something in Portuguese and Pedro's face flamed. He looked over his shoulder to his sister, and there was something in the glance that passed between them which made Sharley more apprehensive than ever. Her mouth was dry and her heart beat fast. If only she had not let Luisa persuade her to come here again! Still trying to look nonchalant, she made to sidestep Alvarez. But he moved too, and remained barring her way.

'Where do you think you're going?' he sneered. 'You're my hostage, and you'll remain here until I bring your husband to his knees.'

Sharley trembled with fear, though she tried with every fibre of her being to hide it. Once again she glanced at Pedro and Luisa. Had all this been prearranged among the three of them so that Alvarez could kidnap her?

'You're crazy, Alvarez!' Pedro's voice was louder than usual, which gave it a strength it did not normally possess. 'Fighting Santana is one thing. But using his wife . . . No, I won't allow it.'

He continued speaking—but in Portuguese—and from the few words Sharley understood, she gathered he was demanding her release. She was also convinced of his sincerity. One could pretend anger or fear, but it was considerably more difficult to pretend anguish, which Pedro was now suffering.

The two men continued their sharp exchange of words and Alvarez lunged forward, arm upraised. Pedro fell back, his anger giving way to alarm which quickly infected Luisa, who in turn started talking agitatedly. Alvarez turned menacingly on her and she cowered behind her brother. Only then did the Cuban direct his attention to Sharley and revert to a semblance of his former feigned affability.

'At least you no longer need to question who's in control,' he said in English. 'If you accept my authority, you won't come to any harm.'

'You mean as long as my husband accepts it,' Sharley replied contemptuously. 'That's why you're keeping me hostage, isn't it? So that you can force him to do as you say?'

'You are very perceptive, *senhora*.'

'It's a pity *you* aren't. My husband will never give in to your demands. He can't, anyway. The Company is no longer his alone. He has a British partner and——'

'I'm not concerned with the Santana Company,' Alvarez cut in brutally. 'Your husband was too clever for us over that. By marrying you he gained time, and before we could find other ways to pressurise him, he'd finalised the merger.'

'Then why do you want to keep me here?' Sharley asked, puzzled.

'Because four other Cubans are imprisoned in Oporto; sentenced to fifteen years each for inciting a riot in one of your husband's factories in the south. And you, fair Senhora Santana, will be instrumental in getting them their freedom.'

Sharley determined to play dumb. 'My husband has no political influence, *senhor*. He is only a businessman.'

'An extremely important one, though, with many contacts in government circles.' Alvarez gave her a menacing smile. 'Nor have I forgotten that you are Sir George Fawcett's goddaughter.'

'That means nothing to the Portuguese government,' she said scornfully. 'And I can also assure you that my husband will never use his influence to obtain the release of your anarchist friends.'

'Then I will have no option but to kill you.'

Sharley felt as if an icy wind was wrapping itself around her. She did not doubt the man meant what he said. To believe otherwise was to deceive herself.

'Don't be afraid, *senhora*,' he said with a leer. 'I'm sure your loving husband won't allow you to come to any harm. If he did, how could he remain in partnership with your godfather? No, you may rest assured that he will do exactly as I ask.'

'Which is?'

'To obtain the release of my friends and to arrange for a plane to take us to Cuba. You will come with us, of course, so that my friends will have an opportunity of thanking you for saving their lives.' He grinned, enjoying his joke. 'But as soon as we're safe, the plane will return here—with you on board.'

'You make it sound so easy!'

'*You* have made it easy,' he chuckled, and turned to Luisa. 'See to lunch, will you? And lay on something special for your friend.'

'I don't wish to eat with you,' Sharley replied calmly, hiding her terror. 'You're keeping me here against my will, and I've no intention of behaving as if I'm your guest.'

'As you wish,' Alvarez shrugged. 'In that case I shall lock you up.'

'Very well.'

Sharley walked past Alvarez to the door. His hand shot out and caught at her hair, pulling it so viciously that she cried out.

'No, you don't,' he snarled. 'If you think I've been joking, you'll have to learn the hard way that I mean what I say.'

Releasing her hair, but still gripping her by the arm,

he pushed her out of the kitchen and bundled her up the stairs into a small room furnished with a chair and a bed. One narrow window overlooked the street, several storeys below. But even if it had not been barred, escape would still have been impossible unless she was superwoman.

'You'd better pray your husband does as I ask,' Alvarez sneered. 'If not, your life will be very short!'

Flinging her away from him, the Cuban left the room, locking the door behind him.

CHAPTER ELEVEN

SOME time later, Luisa came up to Sharley's room with a tray of food. Sharley was too hungry to refuse it; in any case it was important for her to keep up her strength if she was to remain on the alert and find some means of escape.

'I could cut my throat for landing you in this dreadful mess,' Luisa muttered.

'Rather cut Alvarez' throat,' Sharley retorted.

'I would if I could.' Luisa's eyes were filled with anxiety. 'You don't think I brought you here under false pretences, do you? I'd give ten years of my life for this never to have happened. You've got to believe me, Sharley. And Pedro feels the same way too. We'll do everything—anything—we can to help you get away.'

'Have you thought of a plan?' Sharley asked eagerly. 'Perhaps you could pretend to lock the door behind you when you go out and——'

'No,' Luisa whispered. 'Alvarez is too clever for that. He's put someone on guard outside your room. But let's try to talk naturally or he'll suspect something. I hope you enjoy your lunch,' she said in a raised voice. 'The sardines are very fresh—they were caught this morning.'

'They look it.' Sharley emulated her friend's tone, then lowering her voice again, asked anxiously: 'Be honest with me, Luisa. What are my chances of escaping?'

'Not good. All the men here are hand-picked by Alvarez.'

'What about the ones who oppose him?'

'They don't live here. All the men staying here now came with Alvarez.'

'I don't understand how your brother could ever have agreed to go in with them,' Sharley said bitterly.

'Nor does Pedro now,' Luisa said on a sigh.

'Has Alvarez spoken to Marcos yet?'

'He telephoned him, but he wasn't at home. I'm sure Alvarez will tell you as soon as he's spoken to him. Don't despair,' Luisa murmured consolingly. 'Pedro and I will think of something. Just give us time.' Her voice lifted. 'When you've finished your lunch, rap on the door and the guard will collect your tray.'

Luisa went out and Sharley forced herself to eat. She did not put much faith in Pedro and Luisa being able to help her. Alvarez was no fool. He realised the brother and sister no longer approved of his tactics and he would make sure they had no chance to carry out a rescue operation. Even if it meant killing them. The thought set her heart thumping and she tried to dismiss it. But it remained firmly in her mind, together with a rising tide of panic. Calm yourself, girl, she ordered. Losing your head isn't going to help you. All it will do is make you incapable of helping yourself, should you get the chance.

With an effort she swallowed another mouthful of food. How would Marcos react to Alvarez' ultimatum? She wouldn't put it past him to suspect she had been instrumental in encouraging the Cuban to keep her hostage so that she could get a real scoop for her paper. Imagine what a story like that would do for the *Weekly News* circulation!

She smiled grimly. If Marcos believed her capable of such behaviour, he might decide that Alvarez was bluffing. If he did, the Cuban would have no compunction in killing her. It was an horrendous thought, but she had to face it.

She had often wondered how she would react if she were placed in such a situation, and she was fast finding out. She was petrified. There was no point pretending otherwise. She only prayed that Marcos would believe Alvarez' threats were genuine. If he didn't, she had no hope of getting out of here alive.

She walked across to the window. It was only two steps away, for the room itself was little more than a cubbyhole: big enough only for a narrow pallet bed. She began to feel claustrophobic and this increased her agitation. Perspiration beaded her forehead and she found it hard to breathe.

Without warning the door opened and Alvarez stalked in. He closed the door behind him and stood regarding her, his bold eyes raking her body. Sharley tried to retain an outward calm. He stood only a few paces away from her, reeking of garlic and sour wine.

'I have spoken to your husband, *senhora*, and he has promised to call me back. I imagine that means he will soon be here—with the police.'

Sharley tried not to show any emotion; neither hope nor fear. 'Did he—did he ask to speak to me?'

'No. I said he could, but he didn't seem interested. I'm sorry to disappoint you, *senhora*. Would you have liked him to reassure you that he loved you?' Alvarez' eyes glittered meanly. 'Ah, but I'm forgetting; yours was a marriage of convenience, was it not? So there's no love lost between you. It's a case only of the rich helping the rich.'

'You're mistaken if you think that, Senhor Alvarez. I'm not rich. I'm a working girl—a reporter with the *Weekly News*, as I'm sure you know.'

'But with an influential godfather. We mustn't forget that, must we? If——'

They were interrupted by the sharp screech of brakes as several cars came to a halt in the street below.

'That must be the police and your husband,' said

Alvarez triumphantly, and abruptly swung out of the room.

Sharley remained by the window. It was too high for her to see out and, in any event, it faced into a narrow alley. She tried to hear what was going on, but could only guess. Suddenly there was a great deal of shouting inside the house and the sound of running feet. She braced herself, wondering what would happen to her if the police tried to rush the house. She wouldn't give herself much chance for survival if they did.

A key scraped in the lock and once again Luisa came in. She was talking to the sullen-looking guard who had been posted outside the room, and the warm smile on her face made it clear how she had managed to get in for a second time.

'The police have guns and they've taken over the house on the other side of the road,' she said in English, still keeping a smile fixed on her face as she glanced back at the guard. 'They may try to shoot it out, and if they do, Alvarez will kill you.'

'Not unless he intends committing suicide,' said Sharley. 'I'm his trump card. With me dead, he knows he'll never survive.'

Someone was speaking through a megaphone and Luisa tilted her head.

'They're asking Alvarez to capitulate,' she muttered. 'They're crazy if they think he'll listen to them. He'd rather die than be imprisoned for life—and that's what will happen to him if he's caught now.'

Sharley's despondency deepened. If Alvarez realised he could not get out of Portugal with her as a hostage, he would undoubtedly kill her and then himself.

'Don't look so afraid,' Luisa pleaded, still managing to look unconcerned as she picked up the tray. 'Pedro will do something. I came up only to tell you what was going on. But I must go before Alvarez starts wondering where I am.'

During the next half hour Sharley's fears grew. The shooting had ceased and there was an uneasy silence, interrupted only by the sporadic sound of cars and sirens. The house was quiet too, yet she could feel the tension mounting, seeming to fill every crevice and corner of the old house. What was happening? Did the police have a plan to rescue her and were they simply hoping that Alvarez would give in? But they could not be so naïve. Didn't Marcos know the sort of man the Cuban was?

Heavy steps mounted the stairs and once again Alvarez was facing her. Expecting his fury, Sharley was astonished to see smiles.

'I knew your husband would listen to reason,' he jeered. 'Money always speaks.'

'What's happening?'

Alvarez ignored her question and pushed her to the door.

Sharley held back. 'Where are you taking me?'

'To the airport.' He gave her another push. 'I told you my plan would work. When we arrive there, my friends and the plane will be waiting for us.'

'You'll never take off. The police won't allow it.'

'You'd better pray that they do—otherwise you won't see another dawn.' Roughly he twisted her arms behind her and, holding her in front of him as a shield, started walking slowly down the stairs. 'If they try to shoot me,' he growled in her ear, 'they'll have to kill you first.'

Sharley drew a deep breath, determined not to let this man know how terrified she was. She tried to move faster, but Alvarez slowed her down by twisting her arm viciously.

'We walk in step,' he ordered, making sure they did. 'If you want to live, don't try anything.'

When they reached the ground floor, Sharley saw Pedro and Luisa standing at the front door, hemmed in by six men. Pedro tried to move back towards them, but Alvarez curtly ordered him to stay where he was. Someone outside was speaking through a megaphone again, and Alvarez signalled Pedro to open the front door.

As the order was obeyed, everyone in the little hallway tensed. Gingerly the front door was inched back, the crack getting wider and wider. All was silent. No one moved inside or outside. Pedro opened the door wider still, and all at once Sharley saw an armoured van parked at the curbside, barely three feet away from the door of the house.

All hopes of being rescued died. Clever Alvarez! He had it all worked out. He knew that with only one pace between the front step and the entrance to the van it would be impossible for anyone to fire a shot at them, let alone hit them, before they reached the safety of the armoured car.

With a guttural command, Alvarez ordered everyone forward. He continued holding Sharley in front of him, so close that they could have been Siamese twins. She was nauseated by the smell of his body. Her throat constricted and she could hardly breathe. As she stepped into the street, she stumbled and he caught her by the neck, the tips of his fingers digging into her throat.

'Try that again and we'll both die,' he said savagely.

Looking neither to left nor right, Sharley took a faltering step. Alvarez pushed her violently forward and she found herself in the darkened confines of the van. Even here he maintained his hold on her, barking a command to the driver to start moving. Only then did he ease his grip.

'We'll be at the airport in fifteen minutes,' he said triumphantly. 'With the police escort they've laid on, we might make it in even less time.'

Sharley rubbed her arms, where Alvarez had gripped them, then inched away from him. The interior of the armoured van was dim, but she could make out the narrow seat that ran along the one side. Pedro and Luisa were sitting close by, but it was too dark to see their expressions. She sat down carefully and Alvarez placed himself next to her. Where had Marcos been throughout this fracas? Had he seen it all, and if so, was he following them to the airport?

She glanced nervously at the man beside her. If they reached Cuba safely, she hoped Alvarez would keep his word and have her flown back, as he had promised. Or would his hatred of Marcos and all he represented decide him to kill her? Against this was the fact that the Cuban government might not like to have an innocent British girl murdered on their territory.

The van was moving fast and it was uncomfortable sitting on the hard bench. There were no windows or chinks through which she could see, and she had no idea how much farther it was to the airport. Her body was being jogged from side to side, due partly to the unevenness of the road and partly to the hard springing, so that it was a relief when they began moving over smoother ground, and she guessed they were driving across the tarmac towards the aircraft.

A hand touched her arm and she looked up quickly, relaxing as she saw that Luisa had managed to edge towards her, on the other side from Alvarez.

'I must talk quickly,' Luisa whispered in her ear. 'Pedro thinks Alvarez will kill you before we get to Cuba, so your only chance is to break away from him before you get on the plane.'

Sharley nodded but did not speak, fearful of Alvarez overhearing.

'When you hear Pedro or myself shout the word *now*,' Luisa continued huskily, 'pull yourself free of Alvarez and veer to one side—either to the left or to the right. But whatever you do, don't remain in *front* of him.'

'I'll do my best,' Sharley murmured, her voice barely audible. 'But he holds me so tightly——'

'You've *got* to break free,' Luisa insisted. 'It's your only chance.'

'What are you two talking about?' Suddenly aware of Luisa's presence, Alvarez leaned towards her. 'I thought I told you to keep away from your friend?'

'I was only telling Sharley not to worry.'

'You'll be the one to worry if you don't get out of my sight,' he grunted. 'If you're trying to hatch some plan of escape, forget it.' He clutched Sharley by the arm, his breath hot on her face. 'You won't be set free till I'm ready, so put any other notions out of your head.'

'Why are you so suspicious of me?' Luisa demanded boldly, deciding that attack was her best form of defence. 'If I hadn't brought Sharley home, where would we be now? At least this way we're all getting out of Portugal and we can carry on with the fight!'

Alvarez laughed, amused by Luisa's courage in answering him back, and evidently conceding her reason for doing so. But before he could speak, the van stopped and one of the men half-opened the rear door. Alvarez leaned towards it, then bellowed an order to the driver. They moved on again, then backed several yards before finally coming to a halt.

Sharley guessed that the Cuban was making certain that when the van doors were opened they would be able to step straight on to the first rung of the aluminium steps that led up to the entrance of the aircraft.

Her assumption proved correct for, as the rear doors were flung wide, the silvery underside of the airliner came into view and, directly facing them, the steps. Everyone in the van turned to Alvarez, waiting for his order to move. Silently he stared around him, then pointed to two men who immediately scrambled out and raced up the steps into the plane. Next went Pedro and Luisa, and only then did Alvarez make a move.

'We'll go next,' he grunted, pulling Sharley roughly to her feet and pushing her in front of him. His left hand gripped the belt around her waist, and with his right hand he held a gun. Signalling the other men in the van to bring up the rear, he urged Sharley forward.

There was a gap of nearly three feet from the door of the van to the first step of the aluminium ladder, and Sharley stared at the distance and shook her head. 'I can't leap that far,' she lied. 'It might be better if we stepped down on to the tarmac first.'

'No,' Alvarez said sharply. 'Jump!'

Still Sharley hesitated, and the Cuban gave her a sharp dig in the back. Knowing that if she did not obey him immediately, he would become suspicious, she leaped forward. Alvarez moved with her, almost falling on top of her before he steadied himself on the handrail.

'Quick!' he ordered. 'Up the steps!'

Her heart hammering, Sharley obeyed. She still had no idea how she was going to escape from Alvarez's tight hold. All she knew was that time was running out for her, and that unless she found a way within the next few seconds, her life would not be worth a candle. Ahead of her, half hidden inside the aircraft, she glimpsed Luisa and Pedro. Remembering Luisa's instructions, she slowed down slightly, wondering how she was going to free herself of Alvarez.

'Be quick!' the Cuban growled, and dug her in the waist with his gun.

'I can't. I feel faint,' she muttered, and stumbled deliberately.

As her body partially moved away from Alvarez, it made the belt around her waist tighten. The narrow strip of leather bit into her skin, and in that instant she knew it could be her salvation. She stumbled again, and this time Alvarez allowed her to pause. Keeping her head low, she stealthily lifted the prong of her buckle with her right hand, and undid it, using her left one to hold the belt tightly about her so that Alvarez would not guess what she had done. Only four steps remained between her and the door of the aircraft and she knew it was now or never.

'Now!' Pedro shouted from the doorway, as Sharley moved up one step.

Letting go of her belt, she lunged upwards, flinging her body sideways as she did. As the belt came away in his hand, Alvarez was taken by surprise. It was only for a split second, but it was all Sharley needed. She scrambled forward and Pedro threw himself towards her as Alvarez raised his gun and fired. There was a deafening explosion in her ear and then another sharper one. Behind her she heard Alvarez stumble and fall, his body ricocheting backward, and sending the men behind him stumbling off the aircraft steps.

All at once police were everywhere, but Sharley only had eyes for the young man lying at her feet, who had thrown himself forward to protect her and received the bullet which Alvarez had meant for her.

Kneeling, she cradled his head in her arms. 'Pedro,' she gasped. 'Oh, Pedro!'

His eyes were glazed and blood was oozing between his fingers, where his hand was pressed to his abdomen. Seeing the scarlet trickle, Sharley looked wildly round for help. A tall, grey-suited man came to stand beside her and, as if in a dream, she saw that it was Marcos. Then another man was moving Pedro and Sharley found herself cradled in strong arms.

Sharley tried to speak and found that she couldn't. But words were not necessary, for Marcos was doing all the talking; murmuring gently in Portuguese. She could not understand what he was saying, but the tone comforted her, as did his warm closeness.

Gradually reality returned and she looked down. Pedro was no longer lying at her feet, nor was Alvarez, and she wondered if she had been in the middle of some horrendous nightmare from which she was now awakening. But the blood, red and glistening on the aluminium steps, told her that the horror had been no figment of her imagination.

'Pedro,' she whispered. 'Is he dead?'

'No. He's badly wounded and he's on his way to the hospital.'

'Is Luisa——?'

'She's fine. She went with him.'

'And Alvarez?'

'He's dead.'

Sharley shuddered. 'What—what about the prisoners—the ones he wanted freed?'

'They weren't released. The police had no intention of giving in to his blackmail. They merely played along with him to get you all out of the house. Once you were, they knew they'd have a better chance of rescuing you.' A lean brown hand touched her arm. 'You're safe now, Sharley. It's all over.'

'I'm so glad,' she said politely, sounding like a child thanking her hostess for a nice party. 'So glad.' Her voice trailed away and she crumpled into a faint.

CHAPTER TWELVE

SHARLEY recovered consciousness to find herself being carried in Marcos' arms. She felt far worse than when she had been Alvarez' prisoner. Fear had kept her on the alert, but now that it was all over, shock had taken its toll and she was as weak as a kitten. But the man holding her was strong. He carried her effortlessly; as if she were a child and not a grown woman. Still, she must make an effort to move; it was dangerous for her to remain in his arms. He might hear the heavy thudding of her heart and guess it came from the pleasure of his nearness.

'You can put me down, Marcos,' she said. 'I feel fine.'

'We're nearly at my car.'

'I'm able to walk.'

'You're no weight. Stop arguing.'

She lapsed into silence. The tarmac was swarming with people: police, soldiers, civilians—newspaper reporters, probably—and the usual aircraft personnel. Marcos' car was ahead of them: a sleek grey vehicle ready to take her to safety. So different from the plane which would have taken her to certain death. A shudder went through her, and his hands tightened their hold of her body.

'You're safe now,' he whispered huskily. 'There's no need to be afraid any longer. It's all over.'

They reached the car and Marcos set her down gently and opened the door. She slid into the seat, limbs still trembling.

'So . . . . so silly of me,' she gasped. 'I'll feel better once we're home.'

'I think the police would like to talk to you first,' Marcos said. 'Do you think you can cope with it now, or shall I arrange for them to come out to the *quinta* after you've had a few hours' sleep?'

'No. I'd rather get it over with.'

'Good.'

They drove across the runway towards the airport exit and Sharley turned her head and looked at Marcos. How safe she felt close to him. Just knowing he was near gave her confidence again. Because his attention was on the road she could study him to her heart's delight. And how he delighted her heart, though thank God he had no idea of it. His skin seemed paler than she remembered, and there were lines of strain around his eyes and shadows beneath them. She ached to move closer to him, and afraid of doing so, broke the mood by speaking.

'What happened, Marcos?'

'I was hoping you could tell *me*. All I know is that I came home and found a message from Alvarez saying he was holding you hostage, and that unless his four Cuban friends were released from prison, he would kill you. I immediately contacted the police and the Commissioner was all set to fight it out. I was totally against it and we had quite a personal battle. In the end I was forced to go over his head to the Minister, who fortunately agreed with my own assessment of the situation.' Marcos' voice, clipped and sharp was evidence of how rough the discussion had been. 'We decided we had no alternative but to say we'd release the prisoners and take them to the airport. We hoped to find a way of disarming Alvarez before the plane took off. But when he demanded an armoured car, we knew we'd have to think of another plan—and quickly.'

'Did you?'

'Yes—an extremely dangerous one. But by then we were desperate. It was evident Alvarez would never let you go. He hated me too much for that and knew that if

you were killed, I'd carry the guilt of it to my grave.
That's what he wanted, of course.'

'What was the plan you had in mind?' she asked.

'The police were hidden in the aircraft, and once
Alvarez came on board, the intention was to overpower
him from behind. There was a risk that he might shoot
you before one of the marksmen shot him, but there
seemed no other way out. The great danger was that
Alvarez might have asked to see the Cuban prisoners
before he stepped out of the armoured van, but if we'd
released them from prison and brought them to the plane,
there would have been that many more men to overpower.
As it was, it was no easy job. As soon as each of Alvarez's
men came into the plane, they were grabbed and covered
with a hood, but there was always the risk that one of
them might have shouted out before the police got to
him.'

'My goose would really have been cooked then,'
Sharley said grimly.

'I know.' Marcos' face mirrored her own thoughts. 'The
only person we didn't smother was Luisa, and thank God
for that,' he added, 'for she was the one who told us of the
plan she and Pedro had worked out. We decided to let
them go ahead with it because even if it had failed and
Alvarez got you into the plane, we'd still have had a
chance to overpower him.'

Sharley swallowed hard. 'I seemed to have been living
dangerously for a long time, but it's only been a few hours,
hasn't it?'

'Six,' Marcos replied. 'The six longest hours of my life.'
He touched his hand to the side of her face. 'You have
Luisa to thank for getting you into this trouble, and her
brother for getting you out of it. That should even the
score. But when I remember how near you were to being
murdered . . .'

'Well, I'm not. So don't think about it.' She leaned slightly towards him. 'Are you sure Pedro isn't dead? You aren't lying to me, are you?'

'No. As I told you, he has severe abdominal wounds and Luisa has gone with him to the hospital.'

'I hope neither of them will be arrested,' said Sharley. 'They were totally opposed to Alvarez keeping me hostage. That's why they risked their lives to save mine.'

'I know. Don't agitate yourself. Luisa won't be charged, and I'm sure Pedro will only receive a light sentence—possibly none at all in the light of what happened. I'll become his—how do you call it in England—his probationary officer.'

'You mean a sort of trustee,' she said. 'That would be wonderful. Pedro needs someone like you.' So do I, she thought dismally, but bit back the words. Instead she said: 'I owe you an apology, Marcos.'

'For what?' He was surprised.

'For getting myself into this position—and becoming a hostage. I should never have gone back to Luisa's house. It was stupid of me. I knew it at the time, but . . .'

'Then why did you do it? Was it because I'd expressly asked you not to see either of them again?'

'Oh no.' She was distressed that he should think so, though she did not blame him for it. After all, she had so often gone out of her way to do things of which she knew he would disapprove. But not this time. She had to make him realise that.

'I went to see Pedro because Luisa told me he wanted me to arrange a meeting with you,' she explained, and then went on to tell him of the circumstances which had taken her back to Luisa's house. 'I was only trying to help you,' she concluded. 'I had no other motive, Marcos; certainly not to anger you.'

'I accept your word,' he replied gently, and decreased

speed so that he could turn to look at her. 'If anything had happened to you today, I'd never have forgiven myself. All I could think of while you were being kept hostage was that Sir George and I had been responsible for getting you here. That the blame lay entirely with us.'

'That's silly,' Sharley replied. 'I could have refused to help you.'

'You *did*,' he said, flinging her another glance before concentrating on his driving again. 'You only agreed because your godfather pleaded with you. Which reminds me, he sends you his fondest love.'

'He knows what happened today?'

'I should think just about everyone outside of Russia and China knows!' came the grim response.

'And my parents?' she asked anxiously.

'I'll arrange for you to call them as soon as we get to the Commissioner's office,' Marcos promised, and drew the car to a stop.

Sharley saw they were outside an imposing-looking stone building, and prepared herself for the ordeal ahead.

'Don't look alarmed,' Marcos smiled. 'The Commissioner only wants to ask you a few questions.'

'I'll be all right.' She paused. 'Do you think I could have a cup of coffee?'

'Of course. I'll arrange it at once.'

He opened the door for her and she scrambled out hurriedly, before he could suggest carrying her again. But all he did was place her arm through his and slow his pace to hers.

The Police Commissioner came forward to greet her as she entered his office, and hardly had she sat down than Marcos requested that coffee be brought in. He then insisted she be given time to drink it, and also to speak to her parents, who were anxiously awaiting her call. It amused Sharley to see that even here he took command,

and guessed him to be the man who was always in control; of situations, of emotions.

The debriefing, when it came, was less of an ordeal than she had anticipated—more a matter of finalising the situation than attempting to discover anything new. And within a short time she was free to leave and continue on her journey with Marcos to the *quinta*.

Only when she was in the car with him again was she able to relax more completely, content in the knowledge that she could put the last six hours behind her and, she devoutly hoped, never have to think of them again.

'I have some good news for you,' Marcos smiled. 'While you were talking to your parents, I put in a call to the hospital. Pedro has come through his operation and should be as good as new within a month.'

'I'm so pleased,' Sharley cried. 'He saved my life, Marcos. I don't want anyone to forget that.'

'I'll make sure they don't.'

'Do you think I could see Pedro?' she asked.

'I think the police would prefer it if you didn't. Let the dust of all this settle first.'

'What about Luisa?'

'I'm sure there'll be no trouble about you seeing her.' Marcos gave her a narrowed glance. 'After I'd spoken to the doctor at the hospital, I had a word with her and invited her to stay with us. I thought it was what you would want.'

'Oh, I do.'

'But she declined,' he went on. 'She says she wishes to stay near her brother.'

'I can understand that.' Sharley sighed without realising it. 'He's all the family she has.'

'And families are important,' Marcos finished for her. 'I take it you would like to be with yours.'

'Very much,' Sharley said shakily. 'It's silly of me, I

know, but I feel weepy and—in need of comforting.'

Marcos said nothing, yet he appeared tense. His hands were tight on the wheel and his profile looked unusually stern, his eyelids half lowered, as if to hide his thoughts.

'This showdown with Alvarez has worked out very well for the company,' he said abruptly. 'I hadn't anticipated much trouble with our workers once Sir George and I got going on our new ideas for the company. But with Alvarez around, there was always the danger of him inciting them to strike or violence. Kidnapping you precipitated things, and Pedro's action, which showed his change of heart, has also been of inestimable value. I'm only sorry you had to be so involved; but I hope you'll feel it was all worth-while in the end.'

'I might feel that way tomorrow,' Sharley confessed, 'but right now all I can think of is that dreadful moment when I walked up the steps towards the door of the plane.' She shivered. 'I really thought my end had come!'

'Well, you're alive, thank God,' Marcos said huskily. 'Alive and free.'

'Free?'

'Yes. There's no longer any need for you to stay here. You may return to England as soon as you wish.'

She expelled her breath slowly, trying to appear unmoved. 'Is that what . . . I mean, would you *like* me to go?' she asked.

'Yes.'

His terse answer shattered any hopes she had that he might want her to stay.

'That's wonderful,' she replied, blinking rapidly to hide the tears that sprang to her eyes. 'Will tomorrow be too soon?'

'Tomorrow?' He sounded surprised. 'You needn't leave quite as soon as that.'

'What's to keep me here?' she shrugged. 'The sooner I

get back, the better. I wouldn't like to lose my job.'

'That's true. I've disrupted your life long enough. I will arrange immediately for your return to England.'

Neither of them spoke again and Sharley lay back and closed her eyes, pretending to be asleep. She only raised her head as they drew to a stop outside the *quinta*, where Dona Ana rushed down the steps to greet them.

'My dear Charlotte!' she exclaimed, holding out her arms. 'What a relief it was when Marcos called me to say you were safe! We were all praying for you.'

Sharley was overcome by the warmth of the woman's concern, and the tears she had been holding at bay poured down her cheeks. Noticing it, Marcos moved towards her.

'I think Charlotte should go to bed, Mae,' he said. 'She's almost out on her feet.'

At once Dona Ana started giving orders to the maids: telling them to put hot bottles in the Senhora's bed and to prepare a light meal for her. Marcos led Sharley upstairs, his stride long and lithe as he accompanied her along the corridor to her room. He stopped at her doorway, his face grave, his eyes more green than grey, indicating his concern for her.

'Sleep well, Sharley. If you need me, you know where I am.'

'Thank you.' She half smiled. 'It's the first time you've called me Sharley.'

'I'm giving you back your own identity,' he answered. 'One should never try to change a person.'

'Is that what you tried to do with me?'

'Only at the beginning. Then I realised I . . . But why should we discuss it now?'

'Why indeed?' she replied in a small voice. 'From tomorrow, our paths need no longer cross. You won't forget to book me on a plane, will you?'

'I'll arrange it right away.'

Once in her room, Sharley was overcome with misery.
Everything had gone wrong and she doubted that it would
ever come right again. She undressed lethargically and
climbed into bed. There was no longer need to hold back
the tears, and she allowed them to flow, hoping it would
bring relief. Life without Marcos. It wasn't what she
wanted, but it was better than no life at all.

When she awoke, she felt refreshed, and her normally
cheerful spirits began to revive. One of the maids came in
with a tray of food and Sharley picked at it, glad she did
not have to get dressed and go downstairs, where she
would have to face Marcos and Dona Ana. She was in no
mood for conversation, particularly as she knew how dis-
appointed Dona Ana would be to learn she was returning
to England.

Her hopes that a meeting might be avoided until the
morning, were dashed when there was a knock at the
door and her mother-in-law entered. In a long, black silk
dress with an unexpected tartan sash draped across the
bodice, she looked every inch a Scottish matriarch.

'I wear this occasionally, just to remind myself I'm not
Portuguese,' she smiled, noticing Sharley's appraising
look. 'And to remind Marcos too. When I heard you'd
been taken hostage, I was so shocked that all I wanted
was to pack my bags and leave this place for good.'

'But you love Portugal.'

'I loved my *husband*,' Dona Ana corrected, 'and my
home was with him. But now that he's dead, it makes no
difference to me where I live. Can you understand that?'

Sharley could, knowing that if Marcos loved her and
asked her to go with him into the steaming jungle, or
anywhere else in the world for that matter, she would
cheerfully do so.

'I promised Marcos I wouldn't talk to you of your
ordeal,' the woman went on, perching herself on the side

of the bed, 'but he's just told me you're returning to England as soon as possible. Is it because you no longer feel safe here?'

'Oh, no, it isn't that. But with Alvarez dead, I'm sure the trouble's over.'

'Then why are you in a hurry to leave?'

'Marcos wants it,' Sharley replied bluntly. 'He said the sooner I went the better.'

'Marcos said *that*?' The grey eyes held astonishment. 'Are you sure you didn't misunderstand him?'

'Absolutely. And I agree with him. Our marriage must be annulled as quickly as possible.'

'Is that what you want?'

With an effort, Sharley looked up, knowing that if she avoided Dona Ana's face her answer might be suspect.

'Yes.'

'Then there's nothing more for me to say.' Dona Ana rose from the bed. For a moment she looked her age. 'So I shan't have any English grandchildren, after all.'

'I'm afraid there was never any chance of that—at least not with me.'

Dona Ana's eyes grew misty and she bent and put her arm around Sharley's young shoulders.

'In case we don't have a chance to speak alone again tomorrow, I want you to know how grateful I am for all you've done to help my son. I'll never forget it. And nor will he.'

After she had gone, Sharley lay for a long time reflecting on the extraordinary events of the past few weeks. Never had she imagined herself becoming the focus of a political conspiracy. It was a story which, in the ordinary course of her reporting life, was something she would have revelled in. But how different it was to be on the inside for a change; she would never see such an event in the same light again.

Determined that her farewells the following day would be unemotional, Sharley made them as brief as possible. But as Marcos drove her away from the *quinta* and she looked back and waved, she had to fight against breaking down and howling like a child. What food for thought that would give the dark autocrat beside her!

If he noticed her tension, he gave no sign of it. Nor did he seem to be experiencing any emotion. He looked as suave and imperturbable as always. It was hard to believe that this was the same man who had held her so passionately close and begged her to surrender; who had teased her and mocked her and aroused her to trembling desire. 'I love you', he had said, and though, in the bitterness of their quarrel, he had immediately recanted it, Sharley was still sure he was not as physically unaware of her as he was now pretending. If he were, he would not hold himself so aloof from her, keeping tight rein on his emotions because he did not want to succumb to them. But the knowledge gave her no satisfaction. Marcos might desire her, but he did not love her. He might want her in his bed, but he did not want her as his wife. That was a place and honour reserved for Teresa; for a girl of his own race, whose heritage equalled his own.

They arrived at the airport with little time to spare; and for this she was grateful, since it meant there was no opportunity for lengthy farewells. Yet as she stood with Marcos at the barrier, she knew she would never forget him. The pain was so agonising that she longed to hurt him. Yet how could she hurt the man she loved without also hurting herself?

'What is it, Sharley?' he asked quickly. 'Are you ill? You've gone so pale.'

'It's nerves,' she said shakily. 'I can't believe this whole episode is over.' With an effort she controlled herself. 'You'll see about the annulment, won't you, Marcos? If you need a statement from me——'

'I'll let you know,' he intervened. 'Forget about it for the moment.'

'How can I—when I'm tied to you?'

His mouth thinned, but his voice remained calm. 'Time will help you forget. Give it a few months and we'll be able to meet again as friends.'

She marvelled that he could think this, but was afraid to argue with him in case she gave herself away. Putting on a feigned smile, she raised her hand in farewell and walked away.

After a comfortable journey Sharley arrived in a London which matched her mood. The people around her looked as colourless and depressed as the sky, which was grey and heavy with cloud. Sharley looked like a foreigner with her sunbleached hair and her crisp linen suit. But she had felt like a foreigner in Portugal too, and she knew with a stab that without Marcos she would feel rootless anywhere.

'My home was with the man I loved.' How well Dona Ana's words reflected Sharley's own feelings!

'Sharley darling!' She glanced up quickly and saw her mother and father coming quickly towards her, followed by Uncle George and some men who she guessed must be the press or plain-clothes officers. She was hurried to the VIP lounge, her passport and luggage were cleared in record time, and she was escorted to a waiting car.

'Is this all your doing, Uncle George?' she asked as they sped towards London.

'The Home Office helped,' he said drily. 'You're quite a heroine, you know.'

'Luisa and Pedro were the courageous ones,' Sharley said, remembering the telephone conversation she had had with her friend that morning. 'As soon as Pedro's well enough, and you can get away, I shall expect you to come and stay with me in London,' she had told her. 'You'll need a break away from everything, and I won't take "no" for an answer.'

'We didn't expect you back so soon.' Sharley's mother interrupted her thoughts. 'In fact, your father and I were all set to fly to Portugal.'

'What your mother means,' her father added, 'is that you've done us out of a little holiday.'

Sharley was distressed. 'I wish I'd known. If you'd said something when we spoke . . . But I just—just wanted to come home as quickly as possible.' Her voice was shaking and the feelings she had suppressed since saying goodbye to Marcos now threatened to spill over.

Luckily her parents construed her tears as reaction to her dramatic experience, and her mother hugged her close and told her to have a good cry if it would make her feel any better.

'You're coming home with *us*,' she said. 'We won't hear of you going back to work again until you're quite fit.'

'I'm perfectly all right.' Sharley wiped away her tears. 'I was only hostage for a day—not even long enough to make a story out of it. I bet my editor is furious!'

Everyone laughed, and Sharley drew gently away from her mother's hold.

'I won't come with you tonight, Mother. I must go in to the office first.'

'Whatever for?'

'Because I'm a newspaper reporter, and I want my job back. Anyway, it will do me good to get the whole episode down and out of my system. But I promise I'll be in Tiverton for the weekend.'

As she entered the glass and steel offices in Fleet Street, Sharley found it difficult to believe she had ever been away. Everyone came forward excitedly to greet her, and a few of the younger reporters followed her to her office to bombard her with questions, only disappearing when Sam strode in and waved them out.

'Damn clever of you to get yourself taken hostage,' were his opening words. 'Now I'll *have* to reinstate you!'

'Naturally. And give me a raise too! I've always considered myself overworked and underpaid.'

He grinned. 'I want your story ready for the morning edition. We've kept page one open for you and we're giving you a big headline. It's a pity you weren't able to let us have some pictures from inside Pedro's house.'

'I didn't take my camera,' Sharley replied sarcastically.

'Never mind. The photos outside the house will do. We have a whole stack of them.'

'May I see them?' she asked curiously.

'Sure. They're in my office.'

She followed him down the corridor. His desk was littered with glossy prints. Sharley recognised the armoured car and saw several pictures of herself and Alvarez leaving the house. There were also some of Marcos standing beside the Police Commissioner, with a desperately worried look on his face.

'I didn't expect you back so soon,' Sam said behind her. 'I was sending Mac out to interview you.'

'How could I lose the opportunity of being front page headlines?' she quipped. 'Anyway, I no longer had any reason to remain with Mr Santana.'

'So all's well that ends well, eh?'

She nodded. 'I'll do the story now, Sam. Give me a couple of hours, will you?'

Setting out the story helped Sharley put it into perspective. She realised too that she must start making a new life for herself. She must forget Marcos and go out with other men, perhaps even become emotionally involved.

She repeated this to herself many times during the

next few weeks. But she found it almost impossible to simulate an interest in any of the men she met. None of them seemed as real to her as the man in her memory. It was crazy that he could have come to mean so much to her in a few short weeks. We would never have been happy together, she tried to persuade herself. He was too old-fashioned and rigid in his outlook; we would have fought non-stop. But oh, how wonderful their lovemaking would have been! Perhaps in time their physical closeness would have resulted in a mental one? Stop thinking of fairy tales and concentrate on reality, she ordered herself. If you don't you'll end up an old maid.

Somehow it seemed a more viable prospect than marrying and accepting second best.

CHAPTER THIRTEEN

SHARLEY only heard from Marcos once, when he telephoned from his home to make sure she had arrived safely. He followed this up with a magnificent bouquet of orchids and tiger lilies which made her wonder cynically if this was the way he saw her. But after that, there was silence, and she had no means of knowing whether he had yet taken steps to annul their marriage. But she was determined not to enquire. No doubt she would hear from his solicitors in due course.

Her godfather—to her great embarrassment—gave her an exquisite gold and diamond pendant as a gift; in appreciation for all she had done. She had been reluctant to accept it, but he had insisted, saying it was from the company, as much as from himself.

'Nothing can repay you for what you did,' he added gruffly. 'It was no easy thing to marry a stranger and go off with him to the back of beyond.'

'Marcos wouldn't like to hear you describe Portugal and the *quinta* as "the back of beyond",' she reproved.

'I know,' Sir George chuckled. 'I've stayed there several times with your aunt, and we've always been royally treated. Tell me, how did you get on with Dona Ana?'

Sharley hesitated. This was the first time she had seen her godfather alone since her return from Portugal, and she knew he was curious. The fact that he had not plied her with any personal questions in front of her parents indicated how well aware he was that she was not as immune to what had happened to her as she pretended to be.

Sharley had always had a special relationship with her

godfather, and had always been able to communicate her innermost dreams, thoughts and aspirations to him. But somehow it was hard for her to talk to him about Marcos.

'Tell me to mind my own business, if you like,' Sir George went on.

'Why should I? I liked Dona Ana very much indeed, and I adored the *quinta*.'

'And Marcos?'

She took a deep breath. 'I'm in love with him.'

'That's rather what I thought. Does he feel the same about you?'

'He told me to come back here. Does that answer your question?'

Sir George's fine head tipped forward, acknowledging his understanding of all the hurt implied in her flippant response.

'Work,' he said abruptly. 'Best panacea I know.'

'I agree.' She gave him a half smile. 'You always make me feel better,' and she bent down to plant a kiss on his brow.

Strangely enough, immersing herself in her work did help her to come to terms with the present. She did not stop loving Marcos. What she did was to file him into the back of her mind and cover him up with other memories; of parties, of dates with personable young men; even a proposal or two—she forgot how many. But she was losing weight rapidly and there were hollows at the base of her throat and blue shadows beneath her eyes, which made them look even larger in her fine-boned face.

One morning, towards the end of September, three months after her return from Portugal, she walked into her office and picking up the latest edition of the paper, saw Marcos' face staring at her from the front page. Her heart missed a beat. She did not want to read about him, but her eyes were riveted to the caption. His Scottish grandfather had died and he was in London, on his way back from having attended the funeral.

'I will now be dividing my time between Scotland and Portugal,' he had stated to a reporter, adding that the vastness of the estate he had inherited, made this necessary. Only on the question of his marriage did he make no comment, firmly refusing to be drawn.

Sharley put down the paper. The article had not revealed how long Marcos would be in London, and she wondered if he would call her. It would be the polite thing for him to do—he was always a stickler for that. Nonetheless she was surprised when the switchboard operator called to tell her he had already telephoned twice, the second time leaving a number where he could be contacted.

For an hour she debated what to do, then decided to take her courage in her hands.

He picked up the receiver almost immediately it rang, as if he had been waiting for the call, and his voice was clipped and clear, the way she remembered it.

'I would like to see you,' he stated, after briefly asking how she was. 'May I call for you in twenty minutes?'

'I can't get away as soon as that,' she protested. 'And I don't think it a good idea for you to come here. Not unless you want your picture in tomorrow's edition too.'

'I don't—you're right about that. Will you meet me here, then? I'm at the Park Hotel, Suite 812.'

'It won't be until lunch time.'

'So be it.'

He hung up abruptly, and Sharley frowned. Why did Marcos sound so short? Was there a problem with the annulment? Was that why he wanted to see her?

For the rest of the morning she was in too much of a turmoil to do any work. The features editor came into her room to discuss an article with her, but she looked right through him, unable to concentrate on what he was saying.

'What's the matter with you?' he asked exasperatedly.

'Nothing,' she lied. 'But could we talk later? I'll come and see you this afternoon.'

Grumbling, he left, and glancing at her watch, Sharley hurried down the corridor to the lift. But she was waylaid by the editor coming out of his office.

'Just the girl I want to see,' Sam smiled. 'Why didn't you tell me Santana was in town?'

'I only knew myself this morning.'

'Well, now that you do, how about a story from him?'

'What kind?'

Sam eyed her. 'You're still married to him, aren't you?'

'Yes, but we're getting it annulled. And I refuse to write about *that*.'

'Then find something else. Something about his future in Scotland and what's happening with the merger.'

'That's already been written up. Don't push me on this one, Sam.'

'Why not? You work for the paper, don't you?'

'My private life is still my own, and I won't use my personal knowledge of Marcos to get a story from him.'

'Not even if I gave you an ultimatum?'

'Not even.'

'You're a tough girl,' Sam said, half-admiringly.

'I've had a tough teacher.'

He laughed and the awkwardness between them vanished. Taking advantage of his better humour, Sharley hurried away.

It was only as the taxi came to a halt outside the glass and bronze edifice of the Park Hotel that Sharley wished she was wearing something more elegant than her usual tailored skirt and silk shirt blouse. She looked slender to the point of fragility and hoped Marcos would not notice her appearance. Going up in the lift she was surprised at how calm she felt, but realised it was due to numbness. Her emotions seemed to have been placed in cold storage.

With a hammering heart she walked down the thickly carpeted corridor to Suite 812. She stared at the door for an instant, then knocked. She heard footsteps approaching, the door swung back and Marcos stood before her.

He seemed taller and leaner, his skin even more tanned, which made his eyes look pale as crystal.

'Hello, Marcos.' How cool her voice sounded in her ears. 'Am I too early?'

He shook his head and moved aside for her to enter. He preceeded her into a beautifully furnished room overlooking Hyde Park. There were flowers everywhere— bowls of exotic blooms perfuming the air and reminding her of the garden at the *quinta*.

'How gorgeous!' she exclaimed, bending to touch a massive blue hydrangea.

'I know how much you love flowers,' he said. 'I ordered them especially for you.'

'Just for my visit? How kind, but extravagant.'

'To buy flowers for my wife? It's the least I can do.'

'Let's not pretend, Marcos.'

'I'm not. You *are* still my wife.'

She said nothing and sat down, trying to appear relaxed. Marcos, however, seemed ill at ease. He walked to the window, stared out for a few seconds and then walked over to the mantelpiece. He wore a suit in his favourite colour: charcoal grey, and its excellent cut threw his broad shoulders and narrow hips into relief. Intensely aware of the way he was watching her, Sharley moved uneasily in her chair and crossed her legs. Instantly his eyes travelled to her legs and she changed her position, carefully covering her knees.

'My mother and I flew to Scotland for my grandfather's funeral,' he said stiffly, 'but I decided to stop over in

London on the way back.'

'Your mother went directly to Oporto?'

'Yes. But I had to see you and speak to you face to face. I was coming over some time this month anyway, but this was a good opportunity.'

'Was it unexpected—your grandfather's death, I mean?'

'He was ill for a few weeks and my mother spent most of that time in Scotland with him. I was only there the past week.' Marcos' lower lip jutted forward broodingly. 'He wasn't an easy man to know. He was inclined to be stern, with me especially. He regretted the fact that his male heir was a foreigner.'

'That's understandable.'

'I make no apologies for it.'

'Of course not,' she said hastily, and realising how tactless her remark must have sounded, quickly changed the subject. 'Have you done anything about the annulment?'

'Not yet.'

Surprised, her head jerked back. 'But you promised you would. Really, Marcos, the delay is inexcusable!'

'On the contrary, I think it's most excusable.' His eyes gleamed. 'I don't want an annulment.'

'You don't . . .' Sharley stared at him, not sure she had heard correctly. As if aware of this, he came a step closer.

'I don't want to annul our marriage.'

'Why not? The merger's completed, your workers are happy and those dreadful photographs are useless. There's no earthly reason for us to stay together.'

'Isn't there?'

It was impossible for Sharley not to see the burning desire in Marcos' eyes. They seemed to be lit from within; warming her by the heat they intimated, yet leaving her cold with anguish.

'So you still fancy me,' she said with an attempt at

lightheartedness. 'Poor Marcos! Is your pride still hurt because I managed to resist you?'

'Is that all you think it was?' he demanded hoarsely. 'Every feeling I have, every emotion of which I'm capable has been battered to death by you. For a long time I didn't understand what you were doing to me, and when I finally realised the truth, there was an insurmountable barrier between us. That's why I allowed you to leave as I did. At the time, it seemed the best solution.'

'To send me out of your life?'

'To give you a chance to see me more objectively. For you to stop regarding me as an ogre who'd forced you into a business marriage.' His expression was tense. It brought shadows to his eyes and a tightness to his mouth. 'I deliberately didn't contact you after you left Portugal— except for that one call after you got back home. I wanted you to have time to recover from your experiences—to resume your old life among your friends. I may already have left it too late,' he said thickly, 'and if I have, I shall regret it until the day I die. I love you, Sharley. With my mind, my soul and my body, I love you. It was like that from the first moment I saw you.'

His statement added to Sharley's astonishment. She had been listening to him with growing joy, but nothing could make her believe he had loved her from the beginning.

'I thought you wanted to marry Teresa,' she said.

'So did I,' he agreed. 'She would have made me an excellent wife and there were sound financial reasons for the marriage. But from the moment you entered my apartment in London, my whole existence started to crumble.'

'You hid it very well.'

'Do you blame me? You represented everything I couldn't stand in a woman. You were too self-confident, too sophisticated, too intelligent. I knew that marriage to you would turn my whole life upside down. Then came those photographs.' He sighed and looked away from her. 'I felt as though fate had stepped in and ordered me to marry you. But even then I hardened my heart against you, and determined to keep our marriage on a business footing only.'

'It's lucky you did,' Sharley retorted, 'otherwise I'd never have agreed to it.'

'I knew that. That's why I did everything possible to hide the way I felt.'

'Not always,' she couldn't help saying, and received such an ardent look from him that her cheeks reddened.

'Sometimes you broke through my guard and I couldn't resist making love to you,' he said softly. 'Even though you made it apparent how much you disliked it.'

'I didn't like being treated as an object,' she said. 'And I still don't. You resented me having a mind of my own and you wanted me to be subservient to you. You'd still want that.'

'Not any longer. Being close to you has shown me I can never be happy living with a docile woman. I want an opinionated, quick-tempered little vixen with blonde hair and grey eyes.'

'You do?'

'Let me prove it, Sharley.' He came a step closer to her. 'You see, I've stopped calling you Charlotte? I now accept the fact that you're an independent person who will always need to be free. What I must still do is convince you that you need *me*.'

Sharley longed to fling herself into his arms and say she needed no convincing. But the memory of his jibes and— even more hurtful—the long months of his absence and silence made her remain where she was.

'I'm not sure I do need you, Marcos. We've been away from each other far too long.'

'Three months, one week and three days,' he replied. 'And it seemed like a lifetime.'

She was astounded. But before she could make any comment, he put his fingers on her cheek and gently stroked it.

'Is there someone else?' he demanded. 'Tell me the truth, Sharley. I have kept nothing from *you*.'

'There's no one else, Marcos.'

'Then at least I still have a chance of winning you; of making you love me.'

'You can't make me do that,' she said slowly, 'because I already do. I've been in love with you for months.'

Marcos was silent for several seconds. Colour came and went in his face, and a fine film of perspiration marked his forehead.

'You mean . . . You're saying that all these months this agony was unnecessary? That when I sent you away from me, you were in love with me?'

'All the time,' she whispered. 'But I thought you wanted me to go.'

'*Deus*! What fools we've been.'

He broke into a torrent of Portuguese, and though Sharley could not follow it she was sufficiently woman of the world to know he was swearing angrily at himself. All at once he laughed, a free uninhibited sound of pleasure.

'If suffering is good for the soul, my beautiful one,' he said, drawing her into his hold, 'then I'm ready to be cannonised!'

Her echoing laughter was stifled by the savage pressure of his mouth as he attempted to assuage the heartache of the past. Deeply he kissed her, his lips warm and firm, their sinuous movements arousing her to a fever pitch of desire that made her long for greater, more intimate closeness. Her hands caressed him, enjoying the feel of hard muscle and trembling limbs, each tremor of which proclaimed his need of her.

'I want you, Sharley,' he muttered. 'Every part of you; every inch of your body, every particle of your mind.'

'I'm yours,' she cried, tears of joy spilling down her cheeks as she pressed closer to him. 'I've been yours for so long, I can't remember a time when I was free.'

'So what are we going to do now?' he asked, wiping away her tears with his kisses.

'Get married?' she said slyly.

A smile tilted his mouth. 'For the past fifteen minutes I've been trying my hardest to forget we already are, in case I pulled you into the bedroom and raped you.'

'You can't rape a woman who's willing.'

'Then what are we waiting for?' He pulled her to the door, but she held back. Instantly his expression grew tender and he lifted her into his arms as easily as if she were a child. 'With my body I thee worship,' he said huskily. 'Let me show you, Sharley. Then you'll never doubt me again.'

He crossed the floor and she nestled her head into his shoulder, enjoying the steady beat of his heart.

'I love you, Marcos. I love you so much I can't find the words to express it.'

He placed her on the coverlet. 'Isn't there an old English proverb that says actions speak louder than words?'

For answer she pulled him down on to the bed, and as his mouth found hers again, she knew she was finally entering the kingdom of love.

A VERY SPECIAL WINE

As the fire flickers in the background, a fine meal draws to an end. Cheeses are brought out... and then the vintage port. The perfect finish to a satisfying supper.

The serving of port wine is reminiscent of an era in England when ladies retired to the drawing room, leaving the gentlemen to their port and politics. Yet, this rich ruby liquid originates not in England, but in Portugal, and in particular the gray granite city of Oporto on Portugal's northern coast.

Port is classified as a "fortified wine." This means that during its blending, a measure of brandy is added. The port favored by connoisseurs is known as vintage port and is made from rich black grapes grown on the sunny hills surrounding Oporto. When ripe, these grapes are placed in stone vats; then men and boys of the countryside shuck their footwear and squeeze the juice from the fruit with their bare feet.

When the resulting rich grape juice reaches Oporto, the wine merchants and shippers begin to work their magic. Oporto's main industry is the blending and shipping of port, and the city's winemakers are truly masters. They age the wine in casks and then, at the precise moment, "fortify" it with brandy. The result is a smooth, faintly sweet wine appreciated by connoisseurs the world over.

Your
FREE *gift*
includes

Sweet Revenge by **Anne Mather**
Devil in a Silver Room by **Violet Winspear**
Gates of Steel by **Anne Hampson**
No Quarter Asked by **Janet Dailey**

FREE Gift Certificate
and subscription reservation

Mail this coupon today!

In the U.S.A.
1440 South Priest Drive
Tempe, AZ 85281

In Canada
649 Ontario Street
Stratford, Ontario N5A 6W2

Harlequin Reader Service:

Please send me my 4 Harlequin Presents books
free. Also, reserve a subscription to the 6 new
Harlequin Presents novels published each
month. Each month I will receive 6 new Presents
novels at the low price of $1.75 each [*Total –
$10.50 a month*]. There are no shipping and
handling or any other hidden charges. I am free to
cancel at any time, but even if I do, these first 4
books are still mine to keep absolutely FREE
without any obligation.

NAME   (PLEASE PRINT)

ADDRESS

CITY   STATE / PROV.   ZIP / POSTAL CODE

Offer expires May 31, 1982
Offer not valid to present subscribers   BP467